The Old Songs

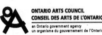 

We gratefully acknowledge the support of the Canada Council for the Arts and the Ontario Arts Council for our publishing program. We also acknowledge the financial support of the Government of Canada.

Cover design: Val Fullard

The Old Songs is a work of fiction. All the characters portrayed in this book are fictitious and any resemblance to persons living or dead, is purely coincidental.

Library and Archives Canada Cataloguing in Publication

Coopsammy, Madeline F. (Madeline Frances), 1939-, author
          The old songs / a novel by Madeline Coopsammy.

(Inanna young feminist series)
Issued in print and electronic formats.
ISBN 978-1-77133-549-2 (softcover).--ISBN 978-1-77133-550-8 (EPUB).--
ISBN 978-1-77133-551-5 (Kindle).--ISBN 978-1-77133-552-2 (PDF)

          I. Title. II. Series: Inanna young feminist series

PS8605.O677O43 2018   jC813'.6   C2018-904372-5
                                                                        C2018-904373-3

Printed and bound in Canada

Inanna Publications and Education Inc.
210 Founders College, York University
4700 Keele Street, Toronto, Ontario, Canada M3J 1P3
Telephone: (416) 736-5356 Fax: (416) 736-5765
Email: inanna.publications@inanna.ca   Website: www.inanna.ca

The Old Songs

a novel by

Madeline Coopsammy

INANNA

Young Feminist Series

In memory of my beloved brother,
Nikola Mitchell.

1.

San Juan de la Pina

THE NIGHT THE JOSEPH FAMILY moved from Meadowbrook to San Juan de la Pina, the cat ran away. The year was 1947, the place was Trinidad, the southernmost island of the Caribbean archipelago, which curved in a gentle arc between the gargantuan land masses of the American continents.

The children moaned incessantly about the cat's disappearance until their mother, Lucille, told them, "Cats hate confusion. They don't like things topsy-turvy. They want their worlds stable and orderly." "Confusion" was one of her favourite words, along with "bacchanal," "shameful," and "disgraceful," all words referring to people who were not respectable. And eight-year-old Tessa soon realized that her widowed mother, who had to make all the decisions in the family, was right about the cat, as she was about so many other things. For every Saturday, when the whole house was turned upside down in an orgy of house cleaning, the cat disappeared, returning only when things were back in their places. This weekly ritual was imperative since the windows remained open all day, allowing an inevitable film of dust to settle over everything. Closing the windows was not an option, however, because the island lay only eleven degrees north of the equator and thus enjoyed a tropical climate.

In keeping with her mother's notions of privacy, the move to a new house in another part of town had to be made at night.

"But why we have to move at night?" asked Tessa, perpetually inquisitive, perpetually thirsting for knowledge.

"Because we don't want "fast" people *makkoing* our furniture and everything we have, and passing remarks," was her mother's reply. In the local dialect, this bastardized English spoken primarily by the non-white colonized people of the island, the word "fast" meant curious and referred to people poking their noses into other people's business. "They too fast," adults would say, with an indignant emphasis, the kind only the islanders could muster, when anyone had the bad manners to ask how much you had paid for a dress or for a house or a piece of furniture. Children who asked impertinent questions would be told, "But how you fast so?" Gossiping about other people's private affairs was called *makkoing*. And since the island was only thirty-seven by fifty miles, scandals and family histories were not easy to conceal, making them fodder for gossips. "Passing remarks," was another common trait of the islanders. They did not hesitate to voice their opinions on any subject, either by muttering under their breath or by speaking in the loud and clear tone that most islanders used.

Once more Tessa had to admit to herself that her mother knew best, since all that the family owned was being transported on an open flatbed truck, and if it had been daylight, all their possessions would have been lying naked on the tray of the truck for the whole world to see.

No one knew where Lucille Joseph and the many members of the large extended family had picked up their notions of respectability. Perhaps it was from the McEwens, the childless Scottish couple who walked every morning from St. Elizabeth Park to the little East Indian village of de Gannes to help out Lucille's mother, Lakshmi Samnaddan-Pillai, with her fourteen children—eleven girls and three boys. There had never been fourteen children all at once in the little wooden house, however. For as soon as the girls turned thirteen, they were married off, as was the Indian custom. This meant that Lucille

Joseph had nieces who were almost as old as she was, for she was one of the middle children. The Scottish McEwens who had taken such an interest in this East Indian family had lived in India when Brittania ruled, and they had come to love the country like so many Britishers.

On moving to Trinidad, the family had discovered that a village of East Indian agricultural workers existed nearby. The East Indians, who had been brought eleven thousand miles to Trinidad, were meant to supply the white colonists with a new source of labour after the abolition of slavery. The Samnaddan-Pillais, like many of the de Gannes villagers, were Tamil-speaking and retained their customs of Hinduism as practised in the south of India. The proprietor of the large estate house, Mr. McEwen, spoke fluent Hindi and Tamil as he had served in the Indian Army in the days of the Raj.

The Scottish couple taught Lakshmi's children to make English food—pastry, pies, and cakes—how to use a sewing machine, and how to live in a western style. They introduced Lakshmi to oatmeal porridge. But Lakshmi Samnaddan-Pillai's grandchildren hated this daily breakfast penance of porridge. Lucille Joseph's children often asked their mother, "Why we don't eat fried bakes or *roti* for breakfast, like other people?"

Lucille Joseph, unlike the rural East Indians, did not make these local breads for breakfast. The Joseph family would buy freshly baked "hops" bread, round crispy rolls, from the corner bakery, while the Indians of the countryside cooked East Indian flat breads on an ironstone griddle called a *tawa*. These breads, various incarnations of the Indian *chappati*, were known as *roti*. Stuffed with seasoned split peas, it was called *dhalpuri*. Plain, it was known as *paratha*. *Puri* had morphed into fried bakes on the island. *Naan* became Johnny bakes. All of these breads were often served with fried tomatoes, onions, and eggplant, or with curried vegetables. Or with *buljol*, eaten by more westernized Indians. *Buljol*, a concoction of Canadian salt cod, tomatoes, and onions in olive oil, was beloved by the islanders, and it was cheap. The dried heavily salted cod, known as saltfish locally, enabled it to have a long life in the tropical heat in the days when refrigerators were not yet a household word. And if ripe fleshy avocadoes were added, all mashed and buttery, it became a special treat, a Caribbean guacamole. Instead of these tasty local dishes, the grandchildren of Lakshmi and Gopinath Samnaddan-Pillai had to suffer this pallid, tasteless porridge.

The McEwens, however, could not be held responsible for the family's conversion from their ancestral Hinduism to Catholicism. That was the work of the Christian Priests who saw a need to convert the heathen Indians to Christianity. The island's British colonial government agreed to fund a school if there were ten children in the area who wanted an education. The price the East Indians paid for this education was conversion to the Catholic or Anglican faiths. In de Gannes village, it was Catholicism. And in the process of surrendering their ancestral Hindu practices, these converts also lost most of their language and culture. Most of the Samnaddan-Pillai family's fourteen offspring had risen in the world and now lived in modern concrete houses in the capital city of Port of Spain, the Puerta de Espana of the original Spanish conquerors. The Samnaddan-Pillais enjoyed all the advantages of this cosmopolitan port city, known as the Paris of the Caribbean, and considered themselves superior to the Indians in the countryside who lived in *tapia* huts of mud, grass, and dung, and remained eastern in their clothes and habits. Outside of Port of Spain, however, Canadian missionaries had set out to convert the Hindu East Indians to the Presbyterian faith, and had almost totally westernized their converts.

The Josephs' new house on Victory Street was in a new development on land reclaimed from the sea. Two of Lucille's sisters lived nearby, and two more some blocks away. The children couldn't wait for things to settle down so they could go and play with their cousins. But Tessa and Sylvia couldn't help worrying about where their cat had gone. He would never find his way here. The woman who lived in the big house opposite theirs, Mrs. Cerrano, had given the cat to the two girls because she was going to the United States to live. Because the cat was a grey colour, their brother Clyde had named him Graymalkin, after the witches' cat in *Macbeth*. Mrs. Cerrano had told the children that the cat was a purebred Russian blue. He was beautiful, and everyone said how smart he was. But he wasn't smart enough to find his way back before they left, Tessa thought bitterly as she and Sylvia ruefully resigned themselves to Graymalkin's loss on their first night in the new house.

They soon faced another disappointment.

"This house so small," Sylvia said.

Earlier in the day, James, one of their older cousins, had driven Tessa, Sylvia, and their only brother, Clyde, in his Morris Minor, piled high with boxes of their belongings, to the new house. Lucille had remained behind until nightfall, when her brother-in-law Lou and his two sons came to move their furniture. Lou was married to Millicent, one of Lucille's ten sisters. He was one of the few in the large extended family who owned a truck; most of the others got around by bicycle or on foot. Lou was a farmer and needed the truck for his farming operations. Uncle Lou and Aunt Millicent lived at the top of a high hill in the district of St. Andres. Lou and his sons, Thomas and Dominique, had gone home after helping to put the furniture in place. The Joseph family was now sitting in the kitchen of their new house enjoying some hot chocolate and bread and cheese. The chocolate was a local product and came in sticks, and, when boiled, it was rich and dark and brimming with oil. It was often flavoured with cinnamon, bay leaves, and cloves, and when it simmered on the stove it exuded the most heavenly aroma. Trinidadian chocolate was deemed to be so fine that it was often mixed with that of other chocolate-producing countries.

"Look at this kitchen," Sylvia complained. "We have no cupboards and no counters. The old kitchen safe will not hold everything."

A kitchen safe, a fixture on the island's kitchens, was a sturdy movable cupboard on legs that consisted of three sections. The domed top, which could be raised and lowered, and in which baked goods were often stored, was made of fine wire mesh, as were the doors of the top section, while the doors of the lower section were made entirely of wood. Lucille's kitchen safe was varnished to a high gloss. It was also finely carved and ornamented, having been made by the same carpenter who had built their fine mahogany dining table and chairs.

Ten-year-old Sylvia, tall and strong, the most practical of Lucille's offspring, was often the one who took over and organized things when Lucille became overwhelmed. Sylvia never minced words. Once an old woman from Lucille's home village of de Gannes had come to the house in Meadowbrook to sell some rather sorry-looking fruits and vegetables, only to be told by Sylvia, "Your vegetables only good for the pigs." The woman, deciding that this arrogant young girl needed to be put in her place for speaking to an adult in such a disrespectful manner, said, in her Indian-accented broken English, "Plain tak and bad manners no good for young guls."

Another time Sylvia told the old beggar woman, who had walked the four miles from de Gannes village to the Joseph's house, "My mother says you have children who are well off and you do not need to beg." This had created shame and consternation in the family, for Lucille had never imagined her remark would be repeated to the old women, whose name was Kunti. The first time the children had heard the name Kunti they had howled with laughter, for Hindi words or those of their late grandparents' Tamil were foreign to their ears. None of them, including Lucille, had known that the custom of begging in one's old age was a Hindu custom. It signified that the householder, who was shedding all his belongings and leaving his property to his eldest son, was preparing himself for the next world. To the Joseph family and their relatives, the sight of old Indians, the *dhoti*-clad men and the women in long skirts, their heads covered with veils called *orhinis*, none of which were very clean or new, walking barefooted around the city in a large gang every Friday, soliciting alms, was a source of embarrassment. Tessa had heard her mother say, "No wonder the people of this town look down on the Indian people. Is only the Indians who come begging every Friday like this. Nobody from the other races do that."

Tessa was confused by this remark. She was thinking about the many vagrants they saw when they went downtown, and they were mostly Black people. Their clothes were made of discarded jute sugar bags, their hair was long and matted, their tattered pants were tied up with string, their canvas shoes—which the islanders called *watchecongs*, no one knew why—were riddled with holes, and their shirts were usually sleeveless vests called *merinos*. Some of them, who carried all their possessions in bundles wherever they went, lit open fires in a corner of the picturesque Woodford Square, and, opening their bundles, produced pots and pans to cook their meals. Others stood on the sidewalks in front of the fancy English stores or walked the streets of the city, begging alms. But, Tessa reasoned, at least they were not in large gangs like the Indians who came every Friday. And why Friday? she wondered.

What Tessa and the Joseph family did not know was that the Indians who had gotten too old or sick to work as indentured labourers on the sugar-cane fields were now destitute. They had been abandoned by their employers and the government, whose scheme had brought them to the island. Leaving behind the agricultural environs of the estates, they had moved to the city to and had to support themselves by begging.

Lucille Joseph thought she would put a stop to Sylvia's grumbling about the kitchen once and for all. "Be glad we have a table to put the food on," she said. "And we don't have to cook on a coalpot on the floor or on a mud *chulhah* in the wall like the Indians in the countryside. We at least have a kerosene stove on a table."

"And we have a cherry tree in the backyard," Tessa pointed out, with her usual optimism.

Tessa was excited about everything. It seemed to her that the world was a never-ending source of wonder and mystery, and she did not want to miss one second of any of it. Her curiosity and impulsiveness would often land her in trouble, and the others would have to bail her out. She was slight of build, and her straight black hair was just like Sylvia's, cut straight across the forehead in a style known as a "donkey mane." She was always on the move and talked constantly so that the others frequently asked her to stop, claiming she was giving them headaches. Lucille said that Tessa talked too much, just like her grandmother, her father's mother Shakuntala, whom Lucille despised.

"That's all you thinking about. And it's not even our tree. It belongs to the people next door," said Sylvia. "When we came today with James, instead of helping to unpack the boxes, you kept going outside to stare at the tree." The branches of the tree were covered with red ripe delicious-looking cherries shining in the bright sunlight. They tantalized Tessa, but she couldn't reach even one of the tiny cherries, and her pleas for help were in vain, since everybody was too busy to listen. The high, galvanized fence with sharp edges that surrounded the house next door deterred her from even thinking of trying to get at the cherries for herself.

"According to the law, we can pick the cherries that hang over on our side," announced Clyde, who was always ready with some bit of information acquired from his obsessive reading. Clyde, a tall and muscular fourteen-year-old, played football and cricket and belonged to the Sea Scouts at his school, Our Lady of Lourdes College. Clyde continued. "But we hardly have any yard. And no space between the houses. Every house jam packed on every other house. Whenever the lady next door shout at her children or when her husband quarrel with her, we bound to hear."

Lucille was sorting bags of rice, flour, sugar, and cornmeal; jars of baking powder, salt, molasses, and honey; bottles of cooking oil and olive oil; margarine; frying pans; big iron and aluminum pots; plates; cutlery; large cooking spoons; her two *masala* stones, one large flat one and one small curved one for grinding spices, both of which had come from a beach on the eastern side of the island; and the *tawa* on which she would cook the *roti* and Johnny bake when she had time on the weekends. She was trying to decide which foodstuffs should go into the kitchen safe and wondering how she would get everything from her old kitchen to fit in this one. In between the sorting and organizing, she took sips of her hot chocolate and tried hard to ignore her children's complaints.

"And why this toilet and shower have to be here, right next to the kitchen? In Meadowbrook, it was in a corner of the house, nobody could see you whenever you had to go. And look at that lane they make across there. The builders only do that so that they could cram three houses where there should only be two." These were Clyde's next comments. He was eating fast and gulping his chocolate, for he was anxious to get back to his latest Zane Grey novel.

Their Meadowbrook house had even had an extra bedroom where her late husband's bedridden sister, Doris, had lived for many months, cared for by Lucille. Before she passed away, their aunt had spent her many hours in bed reading, and when the children came to visit, she had amused them with long and interesting stories.

Sylvia was tired and grumpy after all the unpacking she had done and the frustration of finding places for everything, and she was sleepy. "You mean to say we had to leave our nice four-bedroom house with the long *gallery* in front to move to this poky two-bedroom with a *gallery* which have room for only one rocking chair and one more chair?" she groaned some more. But no one paid attention. In Trinidad, the word "*gallery*" means the verandah outside the front of the house.

Lucille had finally finished filling the old safe. She had piled the table with cooking utensils and any food that could not fit into the safe. Covering it all with a checked red-and-white tablecloth, she sighed and sat down. She wasn't sure if there were rats or cockroaches in her new house. She had made the decision to sell the big house and had supervised the building of this new one when she realized how little money was left. Whether this cloth would be any safeguard from the many tropical creatures that always had to be kept at bay, she couldn't tell. Her bones were aching, and her whole body was crying out for rest. No longer trying to conceal her anger, she turned on her two older children.

"You old enough to know better than to complain like this, Sylvia. And as for you Clyde, you should be setting an example for your younger sisters. You know very well why we had to move. We had to buy a smaller house, because we couldn't afford the other one. You think we still have money after your father died? We're lucky to have food to eat and a place to sleep. You have to learn to be contented with what you have in life."

She knew she was taking out on the children the anger she felt towards herself. If she had not been so naïve and trusting, she would not have had to sell the big house and she wouldn't have ended up here.

2.
The New School

TESSA AND SYLVIA WERE HOME for lunch after their first morning in their new school, the San Juan de la Pina Catholic Girls' School. Running up the steps ahead of Sylvia, Tessa turned the handle of the front door, which was never locked, and, rushing into the kitchen, said to her mother, "Mum, you know what?" She began in a voice of shock and pity. "So many children came to school barefoot." Tessa could not remember any children in the Meadowbrook School without shoes.

Her mother was getting the midday meal on the table, plates of stewed red snapper, which they called red fish, and rice, with a side dish of pigeon peas. She replied quietly, "Well, they must be very poor. They can't help it."

"One of the children, Zorida is her name, told me she living in Cocorico. And has to walk very far, about a mile, she says, to come to school. And not only she didn't have shoes, her dress was dirty and had big rips in places. And it was so long, it looked like her big sister's old dress. I don't know why she wasn't wearing the school uniform."

"I bet her mother didn't have money to buy the cloth to make the uniform. She had to let her wear whatever she had in the house," Lucille ventured.

As Lucille brought each plate filled with food to the table, the smell of stewed fish permeated the kitchen. The fish, flavoured with the thyme, parsley, Spanish thyme, chives, and spices—the "seasonings" that Trinidadian housewives never cooked without—had been simmered in a mixture of tomatoes, garlic, and onions with a bit of curry. But there were always bones in the fish. No one ever filleted the fish they cooked, so it was always a risk to eat any fish, no matter how delicious, as you could accidentally choke on some unruly bone or other.

Lucille became lost in thought. Cocorico was a fishing village to the west of San Juan de la Pina. She had begun her married life there. She said to Clyde, "You remember when we used to live in Cocorico, Clyde? And Darling used to work for us when your father was alive. She used to help mind all of you. Now that we live nearer to Cocorico, I will go and see her and let her know we are living in San Juan de la Pina."

Tessa had often envied Clyde's stories of living in the simple wooden cottage in the village of Cocorico. The way he talked about it made Tessa believe that it was like a village in a fairy tale. Lucille had often recounted Clyde's reaction when they first moved into the Meadowbrook house. He had put his head down on the kitchen table and cried, "But I can't see and hear the sea anymore."

Clyde, recalling those days in Cocorico, said, "I suppose we had to move into a better neighbourhood, a place like Medowbrook, but I still feel a hollow in the pit of my stomach when I realize I'm no longer near the sound and smell of the sea. It was such a happy life in Cocorico, playing on the beach with the boys from the village. I used to love the rotten fishy smell of the beach, and the waves crashing against the shore when the tide was coming in. It was always a wonder to me each time I saw it. When the waves had flattened themselves, leaving all that foam behind, they moved out again from the shore, tired, with no energy left, just a skeleton of what they were before. But soon other waves would take their place. It was like the sea never stopped its cycle of waves rising, crashing, and dying. I found the seashore mesmerizing. I would stare at the boats anchored on the shore, wondering whether their anchors could break off and they would crash into little pieces."

"What is mesmerizing?" asked Tessa.

"It was like I couldn't stop staring at the boats when they were anchored, at how they tossed and turned when the sea was angry."

"You think the sea gets angry, like a person?" asked Tessa.

"Well, that's how it looks to me," said Clyde.

"To hear the fishermen tell of how they nearly died when huge waves came up, raising their small boats into the air, and they were sure they would turn over and drown, it sounded as if the sea was angry."

Clyde could not stem the tide of his Cocorico memories and he continued, "To sit on the shore and listen to the waves slapping against the bottom of the boats is a sound I don't think you can hear anywhere else. And I liked to watch and talk to the fishermen, these old men who had spent their lives on the sea, their faces all wrinkled and beaten up from the sun and the sea. Those fishermen were always mending their nets on the shore when they were not at sea. And when the men returned from their fishing trips, and the women went to meet the boats, there would be so much noise and confusion. The women would bargain loudly for the cheapest price and grumble and complain if there was no carite or shark since they had promised their husbands they would have curried carite or fried shark and bake for lunch that day."

"And sometimes," added Lucille, "a boat did not return. It was said that if the Trinidad fishermen went into Venezuelan waters—it's only ten miles of water between the island and the mainland of South America—the Venezuelan Coast Guard would nab them and throw them in jail and they would never be heard from again. That is what happened to one of Darling's brothers, I remember," said Lucille.

Clyde often ran into his friends from the village who were

now fish vendors in the San Juan de la Pina Market, and who would come down the street once a week selling fish from the back of a truck. He felt sorry for them, for he knew that they had never gone on to high school, and would be no better off than their parents.

"But they are not starving," Lucille said, after Clyde had voiced his pity for his old companions. "And after all," she added, "they can now afford a truck, which is something their parents could never dream of."

Tessa and Sylvia listened in rapt attention as Clyde continued to reminisce about his time in Cocorico. He also talked about their father, for Tessa had never known him and Sylvia was too young to remember much. Clyde told them that they were happy before their father was taken away.

"Our father was smart," said Clyde. "He was far ahead of his time. He sent away for a kit he saw advertised in a magazine and built a radio. He was the only one in the village to have a radio. The night of the famous fight between Joe Louis and Max Schmeling, the neighbours gathered around and sat on the steps to listen to the fight on the radio. I did not know at that time what all the excitement was about, but I heard the adults talking about someone called Hitler, and saying how important it was for Joe Louis to win. I didn't understand at that time why it was so important, that fight. But the fight lasted only two minutes, and then Joe Louis was the heavyweight champion of the world. The Black man had scored a victory that made all the Black and brown people of the island proud. They felt that this victory had showed Hitler that a Black man, the man they called the 'brown bomber' could defeat a white German. So the victory was a defeat for Hitler and his ideas about racial superiority."

Clyde went on to tell his sisters about the morning when two men came, his father's business partners, as his father was lying in bed, sick. "'No, no, I don't want to do this,' I heard our father shouting out more than once."

"Why are you bringing up that terrible time?" Lucille asked sternly. "Do the children really need to know all that?"

"We want to hear," Sylvia said. "Tell us all about it."

"Well, Mr. Martin was trying to persuade him. He said to our father, 'It's a good opportunity. We can't just stay in that little cubbyhole. This is the modern age. We have to expand.'

"'I don't want to have anything to do with that man,' I heard our father say, and his voice was hoarse. He will rob us blind. Men like that only want everything for themselves. Don't trust those red-skinned people. If he was Indian like us, I could agree, but people of other races always think that we Indians stupid.'

"And Mr. Martin said, 'Not all Indian people honest. I think you making a big mistake. He can help us to get rich.'

"'That is all you think about. Getting rich. I hear the woman you marry in San Raphael die and leave you a lot of land. How much more money you need? I tell you, again, no.'

"I was frightened at the loud voices. I wanted to go in and tell them to leave my father alone. I wondered why mother didn't do that. Was she afraid of these men? And after they left, our father collapsed. By the time the doctor came, it was too late. He was gone. He was only thirty-three. And soon most of the money and property he had accumulated was gone too."

"Yes, we lost everything, it's true, but it's no good talking about it now," Lucille said. "We have to make the best of what we have left, and no use blaming those who robbed us. We have to look ahead, and you children will have to find a way to succeed in life. To become doctors or lawyers or teachers. And that will only happen if you study hard and listen to your teachers every day."

As Clyde talked about Cocorico, Lucille, too, began to reminisce about Darling, the young woman who had worked as a mother's helper when her children were small. "I believe that Darling still living in Cocorico," said Lucille. "You know, Darling's husband's family had, since their grandfather's time, been making the *tadjah* every year for the Moslem festival of *Muharram*, which we call *hoosay* in Trinidad. I hear that Darling's husband is an alcoholic, they have three children, and Darling, too, is now alcoholic."

Lucille sighed. "Darling was such a good help to me when you children were young. She adored your father, called him Dada. How the sweet young girl that she once was could now be a miserable alcoholic is so hard for me to understand."

"Mum, I think our Meadowbrook uniform was nicer," Sylvia said, impatient at listening to all those sad thoughts. "I prefer the brown pleated skirt and the white blouse to this blue all-in-one thing. And this white blouse don't have a nice collar like the Meadowbrook one. Look at it. This uniform is the same colour as that dress the women in the Poor House on the Main Road have to wear. And it baggy too, just like theirs."

Lucille said abstractedly, "You shouldn't say 'poor house.' The proper name is 'House of Refuge.'" As she moved about the tiny kitchen, she was thinking about how they would have to eat all their meals in here, for there was no dining room. Their large mahogany dining table had to be placed into a corner of the drawing room.

"And you know what too, Mum?" Tessa interjected. "The teachers give out milk to some children every day. But the teacher in charge looked at us and said we didn't need it. I don't think they had milk distribution in Meadowbrook."

"Why would they give out milk in the Meadowbrook School?" Sylvia asked. "All the people in Meadowbrook are well off, and most of them have cars. So many Chinese and Syrian people live in Meadowbrook. Remember the Syrians who lived opposite to us? They had about ten children, and the mother couldn't speak English. And the day one of the children got her arm caught in the washing machine?"

"And all the women in the house, there were about three of them, I remember, started to scream, and had to phone the father at his store. When he came home, he yelled at them all, because they didn't have the sense to call the doctor or take the child to the hospital instead of screaming and calling him at work," added Lucille.

"Well, none of the women could speak English, and wouldn't know what to do. For the Syrian people always sending for wives and husbands from Syria for their children. They never marry Trinidadian people," added Clyde.

"And Mum, this school was once a church, this girl Brenda told me," continued Tessa, bored with the talk about the Syrian people. She couldn't remember any Syrian children in her classes, only the Chinese boy who teased her mercilessly when she had hit her finger with the hammer and it had turned black. Tessa hated that boy, until the day the story appeared on the front page of the newspaper that his father had hung himself in his shop because he could not pay his gambling debts. Then she decided that she would be nice to Timmy even though he had bothered her so much. But he never came back to school.

"Brenda living on the next street, and she helped me to do everything today. I asked her why this school have all these bright coloured windows all over. She said the school was once the parish church, but then they built a bigger church." Tessa was gobbling her food while keeping up this incessant chatter.

"They are called stained-glass windows," Sylvia said in a tone of great superiority. "But the school is hot and noisy and crowded. I wish we didn't have to leave Meadowbrook and come to this ol' school."

Lucille Joseph knew she had to keep a firm hand on these children or else they would "rule" her. This was a condemnation she always had for any parents whose children ran wild. "She letting the children rule her," she would remark.

"But where you get this sourness from, Sylvia?" she said sternly. "First you complain about the small house, the new uniform, and now is the small school. You can't go through life like this, always finding fault. You will turn into an old spinster if you don't stop. No man will want to be near you."

Clyde laughed, and asked his mother for more peas, for Clyde loved peas of all kinds. He said to Sylvia, "Yes, Sylvia, you don't want to be a spinster lady going to church every day and looking after the church and the flowers and the priest's vestments, or like the daughters of those people who live next door to Uncle Lou and Aunt Millicent, who all unmarried and still living at home."

"You know what your Aunt Millicent tell me one day?" Lucille said. "Her oldest son Frank had liked those people's oldest daughter Nazreen, but the girl's father put a stop to it because Frank was not Moslem. So Frank marry somebody else, and the girl run away. And the other two daughters still there. 'On the shelf,' as people say."

Lucille and her sisters had often wondered about that family. A mother and father living at home with three sons and three daughters long past marriageable age. It is true that they lived in an isolated place, on top of a steep hill in a neighbourhood of only three other families. But the children had all gone into town for a high school education. So why did the parents not find partners for the girls and boys as was the custom of Hindu and Moslem parents? Did they want to keep them at home?

"Do you know what happened to the girl, Nazreen, in the end?" Lucille asked her children.

"No, tell us," they chorused, knowing that some interesting story was about to unfold.

"When Nazreen was about twenty-five, many years after Frank had fallen in love with her, she started hanging around with a Black man from the village below where they lived. She knew her parents would never allow her to marry a Black man. East Indians, just like the whites, were not happy if their children married outside of the race. So Nazreen ran away to live with him. But since he was a married man, every so often the wife would come and abuse Nazreen. She would threaten to kill her, or *wuk obeah* on her."

Lucille did not add other vulgar threats that the wife had used, words like: "I will cut your ass," or "I go send the police in your tail."

"Aunt Millicent gave me the story, and she said that the police can't do anything about cases like this, everyone knows. They could never force a man to give up another woman and go back to his wife. According to Aunt Millicent, it was the greatest scandal that ever happened in the village."

Lucille strongly believed that it was the fault of ignorant fathers and mothers when children did foolish things. "The parents should have let her marry Frank," she pontificated. "He wasn't married and at least he was Indian too, though Christian and not Moslem."

"What is the use of marrying, when men like to beat you up or make you beg for every cent you need for food for the family or clothes for yourself and your children?" Sylvia said, to her mother's consternation.

"But you only ten years old, Sylvia. Where you get that kind of talk from?" Lucille felt another wave of worry about Sylvia come over her.

"I hear you and the aunts," Sylvia said airily. "You always *shoo-shooing* about some woman or other whose husband does treat her bad, or somebody daughter who get in trouble and having a baby and she not married or run away from home."

Tessa got up from the table. Everyone else was still eating. "Brenda coming to meet me to go back to school," she announced, "because she have to pass my house to go to school. You walking back with anybody, Sylvia?"

"No, I walking by myself. I thought I was walking with you. But how you always making friends so quick, Tessa? You don't even know what kind of girl Brenda is. I bet you invite her to come to your house already. She might come and thief everything we have."

"Brenda is nice. She told me which children I should stay away from, the bad ones who might beat me up, and which teachers are hoggish and rough you up. Our own teacher strict, strict, but Brenda say that she nice underneath."

When Brenda came to the front door and knocked, Lucille got up from her half-eaten lunch to see what this Brenda girl looked like. Even with the school uniform, Lucille could tell that Brenda was worse off than they were. Her navy blue uniform had faded to a dull blue, and her canvas *watchecongs* were worn down. Though her hair was braided, a long piece fell over her forehead. Her mother could have given her a *bowclip* to pin it out of her face, Lucille thought. She could not help but wonder what kind of friend Tessa had found, but, at the same time, Brenda seemed polite.

"Good day, Mrs. Joseph," she said softly and with a cheerful smile.

"Mum, this is Brenda," Tessa said. "We going now."

3.
Carnival in Port of Spain

CARNIVAL TUESDAY AFTERNOON. Tessa, Sylvia, and their mother stood among a crowd of people on the sidewalk across from the Queen's Park Savannah, to watch the "mas" as the annual festival was called in the local parlance. The two-day carnival masquerade in Port of Spain, a noisy Bacchanalian celebration, was beloved by Trinidadians and was reputed to be as good as or better than Rio's. Tuesday afternoon was the climax of the celebration. The people could barely contain their excitement as their eyes feasted on the colour, the delicacy, and intricacy of the costumes as the revellers awaited their turn to parade on the grand stand of the Savannah, all hoping to capture the titles of "Band of the Year," and "King and Queen of the Bands."

The Savannah, a huge expanse of green sold to the government by a wealthy French family, was a communal meeting place. Horse racing and the annual carnival were celebrated in the Savannah, and in the evenings, as cool winds from the adjacent mountains swept across the fields, alleviating the suffocating heat of the day, couples old and young strolled its perimeter. Children ran freely in its environs under parents' watchful eyes. Reigning supreme over the Savannah from its western side were seven large stately mansions, boasting an architecture borrowed from many countries of Europe and from several eras of the past. These mini castles, adorned with turrets and towers, each had distinctive crenulated facades. The grandiose structures were the pride of the city and the island, a testament to its colourful past in the days "when sugar was king" and cocoa, not yet devastated by disease, had enriched the island's coffers. These architectural legacies had been dubbed "The Magnificent Seven" by the island's Nobel Laureate. In his acceptance speech, this son of the island thanked the country of India, the land of his ancestors, and England, the mother country, the land that had given him a home, but failed to mention the island of his birth. One would have thought that he had sprung full-blown from the earth like some demi-god, and had not been born on the little Caribbean island that had nurtured him for his first seventeen years.

British colonial Trinidad. The tiny island, the southernmost of the Caribbean chain, "discovered" by Columbus for Spain, became the most racially mixed of all the islands. French colonists had been allowed to settle on the island by the Spanish King. But soon after, the island became a British territory when the illustrious Sir Ralph Abercromby defeated the Spaniards. Britain then found itself ruling a country with Spanish laws and a large French-speaking population as well as Black slaves and free mulattoes who had arrived with the French colonists.

Trinidad in 1947 was peopled not only with Europeans of every stripe, but also with Chinese and Middle Eastern immigrants, as well as Jews fleeing persecution in Europe and Syrian-Lebanese Christians seeking a new land. The majority of the islanders, however, were descendants of African slaves and people from India. The Indians had come to the island because the owners of the plantations needed new agricultural labourers after the abolition of slavery. Some of the Indians—fleeing starvation, poverty, family scandal, imprisonment, or the stain of widowhood—had come willingly, but many had been tricked by recruiters who had promised them lives of ease and comfort, sifting sugar into gold. They had been told nothing of the ships' unhealthy and cramped travelling quarters, the long hazardous sea voyage from Calcutta to the Caribbean, or the terrors of the rolling and sometimes treacherous sea. Many of them who had never seen the sea, coming as they did from little inland villages, would panic and throw themselves overboard. They had not known that their lives of gruelling labour in the tropical sun would be little better than those of the slaves they had replaced. Ironically, an undercurrent of hostility soon developed between the ex-slaves and the new Easterners.

On this carnival day, as many East Indians drove around the streets where the bands were parading, a Black man in the crowd was heard to say, to no one in particular, "H-m-m! Look at them Indians! They out in full force this year. Man, de countryside must be empty today. And don't miss the colours they wearing. Is like they masquerading in they own band."

The East Indians—men, women, grandparents, and children of all ages—were crowded in open convertibles, flatbed trucks, and lorries, all of which afforded them a first-hand view of the carnival splendour.

Tessa had often heard the adults say that all the races in Port of Spain, even the Black people, looked down on the Indians. The Blacks, at last, were no longer at the bottom of the social scale. The Blacks wore western clothes, like their European masters, while the Indian men still dressed in loincloths and the women in long, unfashionable skirts, covering their heads with veils called *orhinis*. The Hindus worshipped idols, and the Moslem men could divorce their wives by simply saying, "I divorce you" three times. Trinidadians turned up their noses at the Indians' strong-smelling curries.

As the Indians passed, a Black calypsonian sang, "*Every time ah passin' gal, yuh grindin' massala,*" at which everyone laughed, even the Indians, for it was a catchy tune. A mulatto woman standing behind the man thought she would add her penny's worth of commentary. These two people were not a couple. The woman was well dressed, but with no carnival accoutrements, only a wide-brimmed hat to shield her pale skin from the sun. The man wore a carnival sailor suit, with tight white bell-bottom pants, a shirt with a large rectangular sailor collar, a black tie, and a sailor cap. Like a real sailor, he kept taking swigs from a flask of rum he carried in his back pocket.

The woman, acknowledging the Black man's remark and showing solidarity with him against the Indians, said, "Why they have to come out here in dey big old cars and fill up the road every carnival day? I don't know why de police does allow them. They can't stand on de road, like us? They only showing off that they have cars and can come to town for the carnival."

Some of the bystanders laughed at these words, nodding in agreement. But others, more polite, remained stone-faced and stared straight ahead. Tessa felt uncomfortable and hoped that the two speakers would not realize that the family standing next to them was East Indian, as they continued to insult the entire East Indian race. Lucille Joseph, however, did not look East Indian; her fair skin was slightly freckled and her aquiline nose gave her an aristocratic air. She had a full head of black, naturally curly hair. She always had a pleasant countenance, and smiles and conversation came easily to her, with people of all races and classes. Most people believed she was Portuguese or Spanish, terms used to describe any mixed-race, light-complexioned Trinidadian. Unlike the East Indian women who kept their hair long, Lucille Joseph's hair was bobbed, as was the current fashion. Her children, too, were not wearing frilly dresses, but simple clothes suitable for watching the carnival, and so did not look like "country Indians."

The Indians used flatbed trucks and lorries for their agricultural pursuits. Their cars were large, old American convertibles, bought from the Americans who lived on the naval base. The naval base—located in the island's north-west peninsula, on land leased to the United States by the British during the Second World War—had changed the tenor of life on the island. A well-paved highway curving along the coastline had miraculously appeared. Neat houses, all painted white, had been built for the military families. Country and western music blared from the airwaves of their radio station, their DJs drawling in deep southern accents. The Americans had also built the precipitously winding road along the island's mountainous north coast that led to one of the most picturesque beaches in the world. The soldiers from the base had run amok among the native women. A calypsonian sang, "Brown Skin Gal, Stay Home and Mind Baby," censored the American men for going away and "leaving the native boys to mind their children." The best-selling Andrew Sisters' song, "Rum and Coca-Cola," had been appropriated from a local calypsonian, who later spent many long years attempting to get royalties for their unauthorized use of his song. Tessa and Sylvia knew that they should keep far away from American soldiers, and had heard the grown-ups denounce women who were "working for the Yankee dollar."

Though the remarks about Indians had made Tessa uncomfortable, they could not dampen her joy at the carnival. She rationalized that even though her family was Indian too, they were not seeking attention like those others. For weren't the Indians only making themselves conspicuous by driving around in those shabby vehicles, instead of standing on the sidewalks like everyone else?

Tessa's excitement reached a feverish pitch when one by one the bands poured out of the Savannah. She was jumping up and down and asking, too loudly, "Which band is this? A Meadowbrook band? Who is the band leader?"—questions that neither her mother nor Sylvia could answer. The masqueraders, goaded by the carnival music were "letting go" in the spirited "jump up" carnival dance. The dance had been invented on the island and had later made its way to the other islands and British Guiana, the only British territory on the South American mainland.

The masqueraders jumped up and down in wild abandon, spun around, or shuffled in time to the beat of the music. Some of the calypsoes were sung in French Patois, a language still spoken by many of the peasants, descendants of those who had fled with their masters to Trinidad in the wake of the slave revolutions in the French Caribbean islands. One band sported elaborate wigs in imitation of the French nobility. Another was made up of women portraying market women called *marchandes*, dressed in the style of the French island of Martinique. They wore flowered crinolined skirts and short-sleeved blouses of white cotton, while around their shoulders they sported wide triangular scarves. Lavish jewellery—hoop earrings, bangles, rings, and strings of beads—as well as the brightly-coloured Madras cotton headkerchiefs completed their striking ensembles.

A "Fancy Indian" band came next. The men, in costumes dominated by enormous and colourful feathered headdress-es, were clothed simply in leather loin cloths, fringed beaded vests, and soft moccasins. They carried bows, arrows, and tomahawks; their faces were brightly painted; and long pigtails made of black rope hung down their backs. The women in short, fringed skirts, vests, and beaded headbands had been all but transformed into North American Indians.

The next band depicted African warriors. Pointing vi-cious-looking spears, their scanty costumes heavily adorned with beads and feathers, the men's naked chests glistened in the midday sun and the women's faces, bare midriffs, and bodies were heavily painted with no concession to tribe or geography. Who cared? It was a people's creative expression, imitating the best traditions of Hollywood movies of Africa of the time.

As the next band, "Treasures of the Deep," came rumbling down the street, a mesmerized Tessa thought, "Why, it's like a picture show." Fish, flowers, plants, and shells of all varieties rose from the depths of the ocean. The rich hues of blue, green, red, and yellow were a kaleidoscope of colour. The velvet, silk, satin, and nylon costumes, embellished with sparkles, beads, and sequins, inflamed the torpor of the tropical afternoon. Venus, the Queen of the band, was a breathless wonder. Wraith-like and graceful, dressed all in blue, she rose from her pristine foam.

Three sailor bands followed, sporting the insignia of the American, German, and British Navies. "Playing sailor" was the cheapest mas for those who could not afford expensive costumes, but who wanted desperately to be part of the grandeur, colour, and fun that was the carnival, and could not bear to miss jumping up on carnival day. The elaborate and colourful headdresses worn by the King Sailors of each band broke the monotony of so many white sailor suits. Then came bands made up entirely of white people. But since the whites would never deign to join the masses on the streets, they jumped up instead from the backs of lorries that carried them. The white revellers were in full carnival costumes, enjoying their mas as much as everyone else. For though Carnival, originating with the French settlers, had long been a festival of the Black people, who used the celebration to imitate and satirize their masters, the French Creoles and the other whites were not going to be outdone by the children of their ex-slaves.

The masqueraders were whipping themselves into a frenzy, the crowd tapping their feet and swaying their bodies to the heady music, egging on the dancers. This was the mas players' big day. For this they had saved up their pennies; worked extra hours; toiled many nights in the band yards, sewing on beads and sequins, gluing on feathers and fur, and adding final decorations to their costumes. This was their shining moment. And milling around in the crowd were the individual masqueraders. Devils, known as "*jab-jabs*," in blazing red body suits, with fiercely painted faces, horns, and curly tails, threatened the children with shouts and long pitchforks until the parents appeased them with a few coins. Robbers, in dramatic black or in bright colours, sporting over-sized sombreros adorned with silver studs, and carrying wooden guns tucked into their silver belts, blew their shrill whistles maniacally. "*Moko-jumbies*," men on stilts, brightly dressed Pierrots, and bare-backed pirates complete with triangular cloth hats and swinging cutlasses were everywhere.

The two people who were "bad talking" the Indians, as the islanders would say, had almost, but not quite spoiled Tessa's carnival day. She was torn between her joy at the carnival and the indignity they had suffered by mingling with "the common people." This was another expression her mother was very fond of. According to Lucille, people who did not know how to conduct themselves in public in a respectable manner merited the very British expression of "common." Tessa almost wished she had been on the back of one of those reviled vehicles, a flatbed truck or a lorry, or one of those out-of-date flashy convertibles, so she would not have been forced to listen to those humiliating remarks. But in spite of the nasty words, she would not have missed the carnival for all the world.

But soon Tessa would experience much more than this "bad talking" of the Indians.

4.

A Colonial Education

TESSA SOON REALIZED that San Juan de la Pina School was very different from the Meadowbrook School. The Meadowbrook School was an intermediate school, which she thought was a strange name for it as it was not in between anything. It was a school that educated its students to their final year of high school and prepared them for Cambridge University's Overseas Senior School Certificate. It was bright and roomy, with separate classrooms for each grade, and the scent of vanilla from its Domestic Science classes permeated the halls. The San Juan de la Pina School had only one room. The building was no more than five hundred feet by four hundred, and it included an annexe at the back for the nuns' private use. There were no people of a "higher class"—that is, whites, Chinese, Portuguese, and mulattoes. In this school, the children were Black and East Indian. None of the children were driven to school in cars, and their parents did not come with umbrellas to fetch their children when it was raining. Once in a while, a white foreigner who did not know any better would enrol a child in the school, as had been the case with the daughter of an American businessman. The skinny, pale girl, with limp blonde hair, was so harassed by the other children, who called her "whitey pokey" or "white cockroach," that she did not stay long.

Tessa entered the school in the third year class which was called the Third Stage, and which was held in a small separate building from the "big" school. Sumeera, the child of a doctor from India, joined Tessa's class. The two girls became fast friends. Sumeera invited Tessa to her home for meals and parties.

Sumeera's mother wore a sari and spoke English with a lovely lilting accent. Tessa thought she had the most genteel and cultured manners. Sumeera's family was living in Cocorico, not in the area by the sea, but on a hill to the north of the fishermen's village.

One day, the girls were told to write about their weekends for their English composition assignment. As they were working, Sumeera startled Tessa by asking how to spell "*jook*."

"Let me see," Tessa said.

Sumeera played with the children in the village, and she had picked up the local dialect. Tessa was appalled. Respectable people did not say or write "*jook*." Tessa was reading what Sumeera was writing, trying to help her to find a better word than "*jook*," when the teacher walked by their table. It was a long table with an attached bench shared by two children.

The teacher, Mrs. Steele, was a huge Black woman, whose sharp tongue scared the children into learning whatever she had to teach them. However, now and then a sense of humour would break through her stern façade like a welcome ray of sunshine peeping through the sky on a dark day. Today, however, she found nothing funny in what was happening.

Mrs. Steele said, "What are you two finding so interesting? Tessa, you should be doing your own work."

She picked up Sumeera's copybook and went to the front of the class

"I was walking on the beach on Sunday after lunch, when I *jook* my foot on a piece of broken bottle and a lot of blood came out," she read, putting on an English accent. "How many times have I told you, children, that '*jook*' is not a proper word? You do not say, 'I *jook*' my foot, but I pricked my foot." Some of the more precocious children knew the sexual connotation of the word "prick," and a faint wave of laughter passed through the room.

Sumeera sat very still, hoping no one would know it was her composition. The teachers tried to instil proper English in their students, and their goal was to eliminate the dialect spoken by the common people. But even though the children learned to use standard English in the classroom—they knew better than to risk a scolding—they continued to speak dialect on the playground. Experience had told them that they would be accused of "putting on airs" by their playmates if they spoke proper English. And, in any case, using their own language was comfortable, also because it said what they wanted to say in a much more colourful way.

That night, as they were sitting in the *gallery* after dinner, and while Clyde was waiting for his best friend Manny to come and meet him, Tessa related the story of Sumeera asking how to spell "jook."

Everyone laughed. And Clyde asked, "Why would she want to write '*jook*?'"

"Well, poor Sumeera!" exclaimed Lucille. "That little girl come from far-off India to learn all the bad English from those backward people in Cocorico whose children more ignorant than they. I feel sorry for her. Dr. Sundarsingh should move his family out of there quick."

Lucille's words were like a prophecy. The next week, Sumeera and her younger brother were taken out of the school and sent to the Junior School of the Sacred Heart Convent, where the fees were very high. Sumeera was soon singing on Auntie Marina's Children's program, the only children's program in the island, and Tessa never met her again. Tessa wondered if the children had been moved because of Sumeera's humiliation about her use of the word "*jook*."

The caretaker's family lived next door to the school. There were many families cramped together in the small bungalow and dozens of children running around his yard. Sounds of any domestic disputes carried clearly to the students, who were often taken outside to sit under the shade of a mango tree to escape the heat of the building.

Almost every day, the teacher would scold the children in Tessa's class for various misdeeds. Most of the teachers were Black, like the children they harangued. They themselves had come out of poverty and were sure that with a good licking here and a push there, literally and figuratively, their charges could too. At the twice-daily fingernail inspection, the teachers would ask any children whose fingernails were dirty and encrusted, "What were you doing, digging potatoes?" One of their teachers, Mrs. Labadie, who, unlike the others, was a French-Creole—probably a poor one, or she would not have become a lowly teacher—used strange words that the children had never heard like "quenk," "albatross," and "marmoset." Although she shouted at the children regularly, she was one of the best teachers in the school and worked tirelessly, for she had a genuine love of knowledge.

When Mrs. Labadie missed many days of school—for she had contracted an illness that never seemed to end—Tessa and three other girls decided they would go and visit her. They began to walk to their teacher's house, but they had not anticipated how far it was. If they had told the adults where they were heading, they would have certainly been forbidden to undertake such a jaunt. In the hot afternoon sun, the ten-year-old girls ventured up the Main Road. They walked past the rum shops and the pool halls; past the large grocery stores and the dry goods stores; past Meadowbrook; and past the newly opened Gem Cinema, where hordes of people, mostly young men who were unemployed, poured out of its doors after watching a double feature of John Wayne in *Red River* and Humphrey Bogart in *Casablanca*. The girls soon found themselves in the heart of the business district, with tall and imposing buildings unlike any in San Juan de la Pina. They tried to avoid the crush of people leaving their offices, but they were almost pushed out of the way by adults anxious to get home after their long days at work. The girls had never seen such crowds of people on the Main Road of San Juan de la Pina on ordinary days of the week. Tessa trembled in fear and told herself that she would never again let herself be led into doing something like this: going somewhere without knowing how far it was and what kind of journey she would be making. Their destination seemed to be getting farther and farther away instead of nearer, and they became exhausted, thirsty, and hungry. It did not help that there were vendors on the pavement selling food of various kinds. Many tantalizing aromas assailed their nostrils. They could smell spicy blood sausage (called "blood pudding" on the island); and corn on the cob that had been seasoned with spices and hot peppers, and boiled in a large discarded cooking oil tin on a charcoal burner or roasted on the grill of the charcoal pot. The scent of saltfish *accras*, cradled in sandwiches of fried bakes called "floats," filled the air. Various local sweets were displayed in stalls with glass cases. The displays of red, pink, yellow, and green sugarcakes—which were really coconut cakes made of shredded coconut boiled with sugar , formed into balls or cut into squares, made the children's mouths water. Brown tamarind balls—made from the sour tamarind fruit and coated in mountains of sugar, which gave it a sweet and sour taste—was a sweet beloved by the island children .Then there was *tulum*, made of sugar, coconut, and molasses.The four girls could only look longingly at all this food as they did not have a penny between them to buy any of the treats. They watched enviously as workers stopped at the vendors' stalls and hurried away with packets filled with food they could nibble on until they could find transportation to take them home.

The taxi drivers were shouting out their destinations—"Grande!" "Diego!" "St Andres!" "Santa Lucia!" "Petit Valley!"—and people scrambled to find the right one. One of the girls, Geraldine, almost by an act of God, suddenly remembered that one of her aunts lived in a nearby street and suggested they should go there and ask her for some water and perhaps something to eat. Aunt Dorothy, Geraldine's aunt, was as kind as an aunt could be in the circumstances in which she lived. She lived in a small run-down wooden house in a barrack-yard, surrounded by many others of the same kind. For each of the girls, Aunt Dorothy produced a slice of bread with margarine and a glass of water, for which they were desperate. They thanked her profusely and went on their way. Tessa surmised that it was embarrassing for all concerned—for Geraldine, for her aunt, and for the girls, who had turned up like beggars at her door.

They finally arrived at Mrs. Labadie's house. On seeing where her teacher lived, Tessa experienced a severe shock for the second time that day. Mrs. Labadie lived in one of those dark and ancient stone buildings that seemed like relics of Spanish times, and that had been carved up into apartments. There lay Mrs. Labadie in a gloomy room, flat on her back, hardly able to talk, for she was suffering from laryngitis. She pretended to be glad to see them, and she spoke as well as she was able.

When Tessa finally got back home home, it was very late. She had caused everyone great anxiety as no one knew where she had gone and whether she would return safely. No one knew anything about her outing because Sylvia had been away from school that day with a bad cold and had been unable to monitor Tessa's movements. So, Tessa was forced to tell them about her trip. She was roundly scolded for going off without telling anyone, for walking that long distance, but most of all for the embarrassment that these thoughtless girls had caused two adults: Geraldine's aunt, who had to give them food she probably could not spare, and poor Mrs. Labadie, who likely wished her students had not seen her in such a humiliating state, an invasion of her privacy.

The world of the Joseph family was confined to the church and their extended family. They followed the edicts of the church scrupulously, and the nuns and priests were placed in almost saint-like positions on pedestals. Lucille and her siblings told their children that these religious people could do no wrong.

The day Tessa was sent to the annexe at the back of the school was a revelation to her. The annexe was a small building at the back of the school, and it was the exclusive domain of the nuns. They went there in the morning to put down their briefcases and bags, and again at two-thirty in the afternoon, half an hour before school was dismissed.

Tessa was to tell the two nuns who ran the school that their car was waiting for them. The nuns' car was usually a long black limousine hired from the same company that ran a large and prosperous funeral parlour. Since this was the first time that Tessa had been chosen to go to deliver the message, she could hardly contain her excitement.

Tessa's teacher, Mrs. Solomon, had said to her, "Now, when you go to the annexe, you must not turn the knob and open the door. You have to be sure to knock on the door and wait for one of the nuns to say, 'Come in.' Do you understand?"

"Yes, Miss," Tessa had said, ecstatic that she had finally been chosen to do this important job. She was certain that she would do the right thing. When she reached the annexe, she knocked on the door as she had been instructed. To her consternation, nothing happened.

She knocked again. Still no answer. She knocked a third time. She started to get nervous, for she was not used to locked doors. Except for the front and back doors, none of the doors in the Joseph household ever shut properly. At the third knock, Sister Mary opened the door. Tessa was shocked to see that the nun was chewing. She somehow never pictured the nuns eating or drinking, or doing the ordinary things that other people did.

"Don't you know you should wait before knocking so many times?" Sister Mary asked.

"I'm sorry," Tessa said. "Mrs. Gittens sent me to tell you that your car is here."

Behind Sister Mary, she caught a glimpse of a table covered in a white cloth. There was a silver teapot and small delicious-looking cakes sitting on lovely plates like Tessa had never seen before. And dainty tea sandwiches. The cups were small and decorated with delicate blue flowers, and she could see small silver teaspoons, not like the big ugly spoons they had in their house.

"What are you staring at, girl?" the nun asked. "Be off with you now."

Tessa thought about how differently the white people, including the nuns, lived, compared to everyone she knew. The Joseph family and their friends and relatives never had tea in the afternoons. Children had a snack after school—often coconut bread, or sweet or salty biscuits with a glass of orange juice—but afternoon tea was a custom of the English aristocracy of the island. Although the nuns weren't English—they were Irish—they were still the undisputed educational leaders of the island.

That night, as the family was sitting in the *gallery*, Tessa excitedly told them about what she had seen in the annexe.

Clyde said, "Those nuns and priests living so well, and they supposed to have taken a vow of poverty. And as for the priests, I don't know about the nuns, but I always hearing rumours about them breaking their chastity vow."

He looked at his mother as he said this. He knew he was being "out of place," a phrase the islanders used to describe inappropriate comments and behaviour.

"Clyde," their mother said, waving her finger at him, "stop right now. Don't talk like that in front of these children. I don't know where you get that kind of talk from. It must be from those boys you hang around with. Don't bring that into this house. Things that the children not yet ready to hear."

She meant sex, of course.

5.
Multicultural San Juan de la Pina

ONCE A YEAR the children of San Juan de la Pina Catholic Girls' School were treated to something that few children in the rest of the world were lucky enough to experience. It was the day of the *Hoosay* parade, which celebrated the *Shiite* Moslem festival of *Muharram*. The school was on the Main Road, and it was in front of the school that several large *tadjahs* assembled. These *tadjahs*, called *hoosays* on the island, were meant to be replicas of the tombs of Hassan and Hussein, the murdered grandsons of the Prophet Mohammed. In the face of these new festivities, Tessa's loss of her old school began to fade.

The procession of *tadjahs* would make its way from the Main Road to George V Park for further ceremonies, and later, it was said, they would proceed to the sea where they would be dumped. For weeks before the festival, Tessa could hear the drums echoing through the night as she lay in her bed. Their strange mystic sounds filled her with excitement and wonder as they brought to the island the mysterious east, which, she knew, lay on the other side of the world. The *tassa* drums, made from goat skins and heated to a high temperature, had a different sound from that of the steel drums which filled their carnival nights and days. *Tassa* drums go right into your insides, Tessa thought, and they churn them up.

Since all the *tadjahs*, built in nearby yards in San Juan de la Pina, would begin their procession in front of the school, the students had been sent home half an hour earlier for lunch so that they would be back in time to see the parade, which always started at noon. The thunderous sounds of the *tassa* made classes an impossibility, so the school wisely allowed the children to remain outside until the *hoosays* had left the Main Road. The street had been cleared of traffic, and many policemen on horseback kept order. Several vendors carried long sticks, which were affixed with a plethora of brightly coloured paper windmills, whirling and shining in the afternoon breeze. They walked about among the spectators, enticing the children with the dancing windmills.

The Main Road, especially the stretch in front of the school, was overrun with spectators, neighbourhood people, and others from all over Port of Spain who had come out and lined the streets to watch the *hoosay*. The pungent smell of fried Eastern delicacies—*kachourie, polourie, bara*, and *sahiena*, all made with ground split peas and spices—permeated the air. Tessa's nostrils were tantalized by the scents of these tasty Indian snacks, which were sold wrapped in brown paper parcels with a dollop of hot pepper sauce or spicy pickles of mango or *pommecythere* called *kucheela*. There was also *kurma*, thin triangles of pastry coated in sugar syrup, to modify the heat of the savouries. And *gulab jamun, jellebis*, and *rasgoullas*. Tessa was hoping that after the *hoosays* had passed and school was over that the stalls would still be open so that she could purchase some of these snacks to take home. Lucille Joseph and her sisters never made these East Indian delicacies—the recipes had not been passed down to them—so their children had to wait to enjoy them when they could buy them at East Indian festivals. Their mothers' East Indian cooking had become limited to curries, *roti*, and the occasional chutney, and they had adopted many of the creole dishes of the island. Foods like *callaloo*, a slimy soup of *ochroes* and tiny soft-shelled crabs, boiled with the leaves of the ground provision known as *dasheen*. Her mother and aunts also cooked the locally invented soup called *sancoche*. It was a thick hearty soup containing pig's feet or pig's tail and ground provisions such as sweet potatoes, *eddoes, dasheen, tannia*, and dumplings complemented with various island herbs and spices. And *pelau*, a one-pot dish of rice, chicken or beef, and pigeon peas flavoured with thyme, parsley, chives, and onions and various spices and hot peppers.

The children's excitement mounted as each *tadjah* attained centre stage. These exquisite creations, ten to fifteen feet high, were ingeniously constructed from curved and bent bamboo frames that had been covered with chipped brown paper and decorated ingeniously with a profusion of brightly-coloured crepe, tissue, and foil. The silver, gold, red, orange, green—all the colours of the rainbow—shimmered in the noonday sun as the *tadjahs*, mounted on wheels, were pushed through the street followed by the procession of religious adherents. Tessa thought that the *tadjahs* looked like little mosques, for they were shaped like the large elegant white mosque that she passed every day on her way to school. This mosque was a treasure of San Juan de la Pina. It had been financed and built by an indentured immigrant from India, who in spite of early orphanhood and adoption by a childless Hindu couple, had reverted to his ancestral religion, and, overcoming many obstacles, had become a millionaire. Haji Gokool was a legend in the city of Port of Spain for his extraordinary entrepreneurship and for having achieved great wealth in spite of not belonging to the ruling race, the class that controlled the finances of the island.

At home the Joseph family had often debated the religious nature of the *Muharram* festival, known in the island as the "*Hosein*" or "*hoosay*" festival. Clyde had said, "It's become like another carnival. It's no longer religious. These people are only wasting their time and money."

To which Sylvia had replied, "I don't care about the purpose of the festival. I love seeing the *hoosays*. They are just like little churches, I think." Tessa wasn't at all interested in whether the event was religious or not. She only knew that the wildly colourful *tadjahs* were delightful to see, and the heart-stopping drumming and the hundreds of people milling about created a day of excitement, breaking the monotony of their ordinary lives.

The mourners—men, women, and children—walked behind the *tadjahs*, shouted, "Hassan! Hosein!" and beat their breasts, while the *tassa* drums resounded. All the women in the procession had their heads covered with *orhinis*; their long hair floating down their backs or rolled up tightly in buns, with their skirts down to their ankles.

The Liakat Ali Khan *tadjah*, the one across from the school, was pink and white. The Patna Street *tadjah* was purple and silver and larger than the delicate Ali *tadjah*. The children could see the blue *tadjah* from Benares Street in the distance, as they waited for the Cocorico *tadjah*, which was late every year. When it appeared, its bright yellow colour was tinged with delicate green touches. Tessa and Brenda argued about which *tadjah* was the prettiest. Tessa loved the pink-and-white one because it looked like a wedding cake. Brenda kept *ooh-ing* and *ahh-ing* about the blue Benares Street *tadjah*. "The blue is like the sky," she said.

Each child picked her favourite, neither knowing nor caring that these edifices were meant to mark a sombre religious occasion. To them, it was like their own mini-carnival, belonging to their own San Juan de la Pina, for no other district in the city celebrated *Hoosay*.

The excitement rose to a frenzy when the two moons appeared. The onlookers gasped in wonder. The semi-circular moons were covered with tiny chips of shiny tissue paper, tightly moulded together. The moons looked good enough to eat. Instead of being on wheels like the *tadjahs*, however, each moon had a large bar at the bottom enabling a dancer to carry it on his shoulders. One moon was a bright blue, while the other was red tinged with white. Both moons were decorated with sharp knives and small mirrors that shimmered in the noonday sun. The dance of the moons began.

Each dancer wore heavy padding on his shoulders, and his head was swathed with a red bandana. Like whirling dervishes, the dancers swirled round and round to the beat of the throbbing drums. It was rumoured that the men had to fast for a long time before they danced the moons. Since the moons were holy objects, the dancers would be beaten if they dropped them. Tessa watched the dance in a state of acute tension, for the moons were heavy and the men slight. "Those moons must weigh at least fifty pounds," Brenda said. Tessa had heard Mrs. Mohammed, their Moslem neighbour, tell her mother about their long hours of fasting for their holy festivals of *Hoosay* and Ramadhan. Mrs Mohammed said that they never broke their fast till sundown—only then would they cook and eat. They were not even allowed to swallow their saliva. Tessa felt great respect for these men and the important job they had at the festival. After their neighbour had left, the Joseph children— who had been listening to her with growing amazement but out of respect, had said nothing—began animatedly discussing what they had heard Mrs. Mohammed say.

"I can't believe that any religion would be so strict that people would have to endure such punishment," was Clyde's first remark after their neighbour had left. "It's a good thing that Catholics don't have such strict rules about fasting. I don't think I could ever fast like that. I don't understand how people could do their jobs, or even their housework, if they have to punish themselves like that. The business about the saliva, especially."

"Mind you," continued Clyde, "the other day in Catechism class at the college, Father Lorca said that some of the Saints used to wear horsehair shirts, fast all day, and flagellate themselves. And some monks still do that today."

"Oh," said Tessa. "What is flagellate? And they would fast for a whole day? That is worse than what the Moslems do."

"Flagellate means to beat yourself with a whip," volunteered Sylvia.

"What a thing to do to yourself!" Tessa gasped. "But, I guess we Catholics have strange practices too."

Sylvia continued. "You know that some religions forbid their women to wear lipstick and powder? Gemma Jones, this girl in my class said that her big sister married a man who was from one of those Pentecostal Churches, not Catholic and not Anglican, and now her sister is not allowed to wear makeup at all."

Clyde and Sylvia went on to discuss how some religions prohibited their followers from eating foods such as organ meats like liver, kidneys, or the tasty blood sausage called black pudding that was sold on the streets, and the cooked herbed and spiced goat's blood that the Joseph family sometimes had on Sundays.

Tessa was glad that she was not a Moslem and did not belong to any of those strict Christian religions that dictated how people dressed and what they could eat. Every Sunday morning, Tessa was the one who was sent to the Khans' yard with an empty bowl to be filled with fresh goat's blood, which her mother would cook for the Sunday breakfast. When fried with spices and herbs and hot pepper, it was as tasty a breakfast as any, and she couldn't imagine being forbidden to eat it. But she had made the mistake of telling one of her classmates about the cooked goat's blood, and Dorcas had said scornfully, "That is so stinky. How anyone could eat goat's blood, I don't know." Tessa had tried to explain that it was no different from the black pudding, which many people on the island ate, but Dorcas wouldn't listen to Tessa's explanation. He told everyone in the class, and they began to tease Tessa, calling her "Goat Blood." Tessa wondered why some of the girls who were also at the Khans on Sunday mornings with their own bowls to collect the fresh goat blood, did not come to her defence by saying that they, too, ate cooked goat blood with their families.

When Tessa told Lucille about the teasing from her classmates, her mother tried to make her feel better. "Well, lots of people eat things that we might find strange. The English people eat tongue and tripe. And the Scots people have the haggis, which is like blood sausage made of the heart, liver, and lungs of a sheep. So don't worry with those ignorant children." "Ignorant" was another favourite word of Lucille's.

Tessa soon discovered that religion and fasting did not prevent people from doing bad things. The next day, Tessa, Sylvia, and their mother went to the village of Cocorico to visit their Mother's old helper, Darling. It was customary after the *hoosay* festival for Darling to entertain her former employer and her children with sweets made for the festival. And after the visit, she would send them home with a container of *sawine*. This traditional dish made during the Moslem festivals was something the children looked forward to. It was a drink made of milk and parched vermicelli noodles, raisins, and almonds, and flavoured with cloves, cinnamon, and cardamom.

Clyde had often criticized his mother for visiting Darling. He said that neither Darling's place nor her food would be clean since she was now an alcoholic. But Lucille said that Darling usually stopped drinking when the Moslem fasting days were on, and would keep the fast. In spite of Clyde's objections, Lucille felt that she was obligated to keep in touch with Darling, and visiting her was one of her acts of charity. She would hurt Darling's feelings if she stopped going. She could not bring herself to cast Darling aside, to snub her and break off their old relationship.

Darling's wooden shack was located down a dirt alley and was surrounded by many others of the same kind. Behind the village was a hilly, forested area. Though they had been there before, Tessa always felt a darkness and gloom envelop her as they walked down the alley. The unshaven men sitting outside their huts drinking and smoking, wearing only singlets and shorts, always scared her. There were never saw any women with them and she wondered only the men sat outside in the afternoons "catching the breeze."

As they approached Darling's house, Tessa's fears came to faruition. A woman's loud screams were heard coming from the back of the shack next door. Just then a man came running out from behind the shack and into the forest with a bloody cutlass in his hand. It was Darling's neighbour, Omar Khan. The yard in front of the small shack was soon filled with neighbours. Some of the men ran after him, intending to bring him to justice, but the small wiry man eluded them, and they were forced to come back. Omar Khan was a man who made his living by cutting and burning wood for charcoal, and he was at home in the forest. A young man was also seen running away. "Omar Khan must a find his daughter with dis boy, so he kill her. He feel it was shameful to find them here, behind the cow pen doing what he see them doing, so he kill her," , Darling whispered to Lucille.

Lucille and the children were too upset by what they had seen, and they didn't want to linger. Lucille told Darling that they would not stay. The police would be there soon and they did not want to have to answer any questions. As well, Lucille suggested to Darling, "Quick, quick, send one of your sons. Jamal is old enough; he must know where the child mother working. He must tell her what happened to her only daughter."

The mother, Hassina, worked as a servant for one of the rich Syrian families across the main road from the village. Darlene nodded, and sent Jamal there right away.

The use of a cutlass to commit murder was a common oc-currence on the island. Most men owned cutlasses, and every household usually had one. Strong, finely constructed cutlasses were a source of pride for their owners, for the strength of the handle and the cut of the blade were not all the same. Cutlasses were kept sharpened as they were used daily for cutting grass, cane, or coconuts. They were dangerous weapons and were often used among the East Indians for wife killings. It was common knowledge that in the days of indentureship many of the English, Irish, and Scottish overseers on the estates would sexually abuse the East Indian women working in the fields and the aggrieved husbands would not hesitate to go after the offenders with their cutlasses. The "drivers," usually tall muscular Indian men selected to "drive" the workers, would also abuse their positions. Unfaithful wives, too, often met the same fate.

Clyde was incensed when Lucille and the girls arrived home and told him what they had witnessed.

"I suppose now you will realize that keeping friendly with that woman is a waste of time. And as for going back there to that backward village, where people have not progressed through education and are not trying to better themselves like everyone else in this time of prosperity, is dangerous too," Clyde railed.

But Tessa and Sylvia had asked Darling about her neighbour. Wasn't Omar Khan the man who had been dancing the moon at the *hoosay*? Tessa had heard one of the Moslem girls in her class say that Omar Khan was one of the best dancers of the moon that people had ever seen.

As they went over the story of the murder, Tessa was puzzled. "I thought they had to fast before they danced the moon. That dancing the moon is a holy act," she said.

"It just goes to show," said Clyde, "how religion doesn't always help people to live good lives. Fasting and religious rituals alone do not solve problems that come up in life. The father felt that the girl was disgracing the family by doing whatever she was doing with that boy, and so he had to preserve the honour of the family by killing her."

"But what were they doing?" Tessa persisted. "Everybody says 'doing it'—but what does that mean?"

No one volunteered to explain. All Tessa got from the whole incident was that it was an "honour killing." And that the honour of your family was more important than the life of your child.

This was Clyde's explanation. As for Lucille, she was quiet. She could not put the picture of the girl covered in blood, with gaping wounds all over her body, out of her mind. She regretted that she had not taken her children away immediately and that they had not been spared the gruesome scene.

Tessa soon realized that moving to San Juan de la Pina meant that they had "come down in the world." They had left Meadowbrook, an upper-middle-class neighbourhood, and a house with separate servants' quarters at the back for this cramped two-bedroom bungalow jammed up on to others of the same kind. Tessa never remembered any servants living in their Meadowbrook house, however; the death of their father had meant that servants were out of the question. The servants' quarters had been occupied by a seamstress who paid her mother a monthly rent.

Their new house in San Juan de la Pina was part of a new development, and all the houses were concrete bungalows, tastefully painted. Although the front yards were miniscule, most people had planted the red blood poinsettia, which bloomed at Christmas, and hibiscuses of red, white, purple, and yellow. Their fences dripped with the delicate, multitudinous blossoms of the purple bougainvillea. Ixoras and roses filled their front gardens, and baskets of cascading ferns overhung the eaves of their galleries. These baskets created privacy and coolness when the homeowners sat there in the evenings. Everyone had neat, low brick fences that were whitewashed every Christmas.

Their street was called Victory Street, since the land had been developed after the war had been won. Victory Street had two advantages over their street in Meadowbrook. One was that they had easy access to Silk Cotton Road, where they could glimpse the sea between the houses along the shoreline. Another was that Victory Street provided them with a clear view of the Northern Range, its beautiful blue-green hills shimmering in the distance. At the top of one of these hills was an old fort with ancient green cannons, mementoes of the European powers' vicious struggle for supremacy of the little island, while bloodthirsty pirates roamed the seas below. From the heights of Fort George, where the Joseph children had been taken on picnics many times, they had an unrivalled view of the western edge of the town and the sea glimmering beneath the azure sky.

"But," Clyde asked his sisters, "do you know that Fort George never saw action as a real fort? It was built by the British in 1804 after they had captured the island from the Spanish, but it was mainly used for storing the valuables of the rich people when they thought there was trouble, like a slave uprising."

Victory Street, inhabited by respectable middle-class people of many races, was bounded one side by Silk Cotton Road which bordered the sea, and on the other by Main Road. Main Road was a virtual marketplace with greengrocers' stalls called provision shops, grocery stores, and parlours, which sold varieties of edibles such as candy, cakes, bread, and soft drinks. Nearer to the centre of the Main Road, far away from Victory Street, were dens of iniquity: rum shops, gambling clubs, and pool halls. Because of its commercial nature, Main Road was prey to all manner of vulgar goings-on, remaining noisy and alive till all hours of the morning. Because of this street, San Juan de la Pina became known as "the town that never sleeps." On weekends, at four in the morning, hungry all-night partiers from all over the city would descend on the centre of San Juan de la Pina's Main Road, seeking out a "bake and shark" sandwich, hot fried shark and the fried, crispy flatbread known as "bake."

Lucille Joseph never allowed her daughters to go to the Main Road alone as she did not consider it safe. At the corner of Victory Street and Main Road was a huge, white, decrepit, two-storey dwelling, in which a multitude of families lived. Respectable people might have living there, but one woman gave the whole building a bad name. She was known as Wabeen, the name of a common freshwater fish. This name was also used for women of the night. Now old and unattractive, she had taken to drink and was seen and heard all over the neighbourhood singing and cussing all day and late into the night. She was a woman with a wasted body and a heavily lined face, but she often had a half-smile on her face, as though she had many secrets. She was toothless, wore shapeless faded cotton dresses that hung loosely off her shoulders, and she was generally considered to be harmless. But Tessa had never encountered anyone like Wabeen in Meadowbrook.

The only times Tessa remembered being scared in Meadowbrook were whenever she and Sylvia ran into American soldiers who often stopped them as they walked to school and offered them chewing gum. There were army barracks nearby, so the soldiers were often on the streets. But the children had been warned never to accept gum from the soldiers and never to talk to them. The day a young soldier followed them on their way to school, the children were terrified. They ran back home to tell their mother. Their cousin James was visiting, and he went out to the gate to ask the soldier why he was following the two little girls. At this, the soldier began to cry, and said that he was only trying to be friendly and that missed his own little sisters whom he had left behind in the States.

After he had spoken to the young American, James explained to Lucille that the soldier was a young boy, no more than seventeen, that he had left his family and little sisters far away, and that he was probably looking for another family because he was lonely.

"All the same," Lucille said, "you can't trust any strange young man around your family and your little girls. It's dangerous."

On the main road of San Juan de la Pina, there were other homeless people wandering around, in addition to Wabeen. A man known as Misery hung around the street all day, writing on the pavement with a piece of charcoal from one end of the long street to the other. He wrote in large curving cursive strokes, which meant that he had gone to school. He, like Wabeen, was never considered dangerous. No one was afraid of him; his expression was very calm and peaceful, and he never spoke. He was a good-looking man, tall and slim with piercing black eyes, a full head of black curly hair, and a bushy black beard. Tessa thought he looked like Jesus Christ. No one knew the story behind this man, but he was allowed to continue with his pavement writing since he didn't pose a threat to anyone. His clothes were ragged and dirty, his pants were held up with string, and everything he wore was covered in the charcoal dust from his writing.

Chauffeur was another character on the main road. He drove an imaginary car all day long, turning corners on his imaginary steering wheel, stepping on his imaginary brakes, making the whirring sound of a motor car, and changing gears frequently. According to rumour, a curse had been put on Chauffeur so that he would drive a car the rest of his life. Like Misery, no one knew what had caused him to become like that. San Juan de la Pina was an interesting place indeed, Tessa thought—far more diverse than Meadowbrook.

All the children gave Misery a wide berth. But Tessa was always wondering about his writing. Clyde speculated that perhaps he was an expelled high school student who chose to continue his studies by writing on the pavement all day long. When Tessa and Sylvia had to go on an errand on Main Road after school, Misery would still be there, engrossed in writing his tomes on the pavement.

One afternoon, when she was walking home from school with Brenda and Sylvia, Tessa she stopped to read what Misery had written. It was a memory that would stay with her for the rest of her life. Absorbed in trying to make sense of his words and sentences, Tessa hadn't notice when Misery walked over and stood right beside her. But Sylvia and Brenda did notice and terrified, they ran up to her and, each one grabbing an arm, pulled her away. They started to run, dragging Tessa with them.

"What happen to you, Tessa? You want him to follow us home or what?" Sylvia scolded, as soon as she felt that they had gotten far enough away.

"I just wanted to read what he had written," said Tessa. It suddenly dawned on her that what she had done was a dangerous thing. "He always writing all day long. I was curious, that's all. Nobody ever talks to him, nobody reads what he writes. I wonder where he gets his charcoal from, to write all day long like that."

"But why you bothering your head about Misery, Tessa? Nobody else worrying about him. He's a vagrant. We should just leave him alone. The police don't trouble him, and I bet is Miss Dolly who does give him the charcoal from her coal shop for him to write on the pavement. Why you have to concern yourself about things like that, Tessa? You real funny, yes," said Brenda.

Tessa had to endure further humiliation when Sylvia reported to the family what she had done. Her mother looked at her with a scared expression on her face, one Tessa was to see many times as the years went by, whenever Lucille found herself puzzling over the actions of her younger daughter. According to Lucille, Tessa seemed to want so much from the world and she was not willing to wait patiently for things to take their natural course. Her sunny and naïve disposition made her believe that nothing could harm her or thwart her dreams, and Lucille was convinced this meant that Tessa would face a dangerous future. She sometimes wondered why Tessa was so different from her other children. Had a *douen* or *obeah* woman put a curse on her, like in the island folkore? Why would Tessa do such a strange a thing as follow this vagrant, this man of the street? But where would she have been exposed to an *obeah* woman? Lucille pondered. Tessa's problem was, like Lucille's, one of trusting too much, of being unable to recognize evil even if it was right in front of her eyes. Lucille sighed. *Douens* and *obeah* women belonged to the island's past, to the folklore that emanated out of the deep darkness of their rain-forested hills. It did not exist in this modern city of Port of Spain, in this suburb of San Juan de la Pina. And Lucille no more believed in the folk legends of the island than she believed in the curses of fairy tales. She thought of herself as a modern civilized woman. Though she told herself repeatedly that she didn't believe in *obeah* or black magic, in the back of her mind she wondered if a curse had been placed on her family. It would certainly not have come from her side of the family; she was sure of that. But she hated her mother-in-law for what she had done to her, and so Lucille pondered that perhaps the bad blood on that side of the family had tainted one of her children. But, Lucille reflected, as long as a person prayed and trusted in God and the saints, what was there to fear? Except that she knew one could never predict the way one's children might turn out. Hadn't she seen it among the neighbours' children, people who were at church more than once a week, and whose children had ended up in jail, or had to run away to Venezuela and hide there because they were wanted for murder or robbery, humiliating their respectable church-going parents? Lucille sighed once more and decided that she would have to say a special prayer tonight for her over-imaginative daughter.

6.
Racial Vendettas

I T WAS A SUNDAY AFTERNOON during a dull time of the
year. It was not Christmas, not *hoosay*, not Carnival, neither
Easter nor August vacation. But it was an afternoon that
was to remain in Tessa's mind as one of the landmarks of her
childhood. Tessa and Sylvia were walking to their Aunt Violet's
house, which was nine blocks away. They were wearing their
Christmas dresses, Tessa in pink, Sylvia in blue. They got only
one or two "good dresses" for the year, and they usually wore
them on Sundays.

There was nothing for the girls to do in San Juan de la Pina
on Sunday afternoons. The boys played cricket and football
on empty lots. But it was inconceivable that the girls would
join in such games, and their front and back yards were so
small that running and playing there was not much fun. Tessa
missed Meadowbrook, especially its parks and squares and
the bandstand where the police band played music on Sunday
afternoons. Not only was San Juan de la Pina devoid of parks
and squares, none of the neighbours threw birthday parties
for their children as they did in Meadowbrook, where Tessa
and Sylvia could pin the tail on the donkey and play musical
chairs and win prizes.

A visit to Aunt Violet or Aunt Clarissa was all that they
could look forward to on a Sunday afternoon. To visit Aunt
Clarissa, whose husband owned a spacious and prosperous
general store, was not easy, since their large two-storied house

was like a fortress barricaded by a tall iron fence and a chain-locked gate. Visitors had to stand at the gate and ring the bell. They were the only people Tessa knew who had a doorbell, or a gate bell, really. Whenever anyone rang the bell, the two fierce dogs guarding the compound would have to be tied up before the gate could be opened.

Tessa and Sylvia were almost at their Aunt Violet's house when a heavy rain began. They took refuge under the eaves of a closed shop. This shop, like all the others in the island, was a rectangular wooden frame building with a triangular peaked roof, covered with galvanized iron, that projected into a wide overhang. Most people sheltered under these overhangs when the rain fell, since very few people owned umbrellas. Soon two Black boys, taller and bigger than Tessa and Sylvia, joined them. The boys were ragged and dirty. Their short pants were torn in many places, and the sleeves of their shirts were hanging down—the shoulder seams had come apart and had not been mended. They looked fierce and dangerous. They must have come from the squatter's village in the nearby hills. Many of these squatters had immigrated, legally or otherwise, from what the Trinidadians scornfully called the "small islands," forgetting that their own Trinidad was only a dot on the map of the world. Tessa always thought that these squatters must be forest people because their eyes were wild and strange, and their hair was matted and unkempt. They looked different from the Black people of San Juan de la Pina, most of whom kept their hair trimmed neatly and their clothes clean and in good order. As soon as the boys came to shelter under the shop, Tessa and Sylvia began to worry. They couldn't leave because the rain had become a downpour, but they tried to keep as far away from the boys as they could.

Sunday afternoon in San Juan de la Pina was a hot, quiet, sleepy time. The ninety-degree Fahrenheit temperature did not encourage strenuous activity outside unless it was absolutely necessary. And after their customary Sunday midday meal of stewed chicken, crab, and *callaloo*, as well as rice and pigeon peas *pelau*, an afternoon siesta was the common custom. That Sunday afternoon, there was no one around except these four children sheltering from the rain under the closed shop.

The girls soon found themselves in trouble.

"Hey *coolie* gals," the boys started out, "whey all yuh going, all dressed up? All yuh tink yuh better than we? We go show yuh."

The word "*coolie*," which was used on the island to refer to the Indians, was considered derogatory. The boys began to swear and curse in language the girls never heard at home. Tessa and Sylvia had been taught to ignore taunts, to remain quiet in the face of verbal insults. Their silence incensed their attackers. The boys soon moved on to physical threats. Tessa and Sylvia were helpless and confused. They were not used to fighting, especially with boys. When the girls were angry with each other they would indulge in fisticuffs, pulling hair or scratching with their nails. But their mother's threat to pack up and go, leaving them alone in the house, so frightened them that they learned to settle their disagreements without resorting to the physical violence. Since they had no father, the thought of what would happen to them without even a mother to protect them was not even worth contemplating. And their mother always preached the virtue of peace. She didn't like confrontations, and she usually walked away from them. Her children too, learned to avoid quarrels and fights. Sometimes the family would hear the neighbours shouting and cussing at each other, and Lucille would close her window in disgust. "The whole world shouldn't hear about your problems," she would admonish her children. "That is low-class behaviour." And Clyde was never one to play-fight with his sisters, like other boys. Neither did he tease them. Tessa and Sylvia had no experience in dealing with these tough-looking assailants.

A severe kick sent Tessa reeling to the floor. Sylvia was punched in the face, unable to help her sister. The blows showed no sign of letting up, and there was no one to hear their screams. There was not another person, man or boy, woman or child, no inquisitive Granny peering through a window on this hot and silent Sunday afternoon, no passersby who might save them. They were not even able to run away because the boys soon had them down on the ground, and they were pummelling them mercilessly. Then, as if by some miracle, Aunt Violet's eldest son, Trevor, suddenly came around the corner on his bicycle.

"What you boys doing to these lil' girls?" Trevor scolded the boys sternly. "Why you don't leave them alone? You can't see they so much smaller than you?"

The boys did not wait to answer but scurried away. They could not help but be intimidated by this tall and muscular eighteen-year-old. Trevor was a formidable opponent; he played football, cricket, and water polo at the prestigious St. Francis College, where sports were as important as academics, in the best English grammar school tradition. No sooner had he recognized what was happening than he jumped down from his sporty ten-speed bicycle, only to find out that the girls being so viciously attacked were his cousins.

The girls arrived at their aunt's house dirtied and bloodied and sobbing helplessly.

Tessa was sure this was just an unlucky experience. Yet some weeks later she had to endure another random act of aggression. One morning she had ridden her bike to a nearby shop to buy fresh hops bread for breakfast, and was on her way home. A Black boy deliberately swerved into her path, knocking her and the bread into the open drain. Once more she arrived home weeping, but all the comfort she got was the helpless look on the faces of Sylvia, Clyde, and her mother. The expression of satisfaction on the face of the Black boy had puzzled Tessa for a long time. What vendetta was he satisfying, and why he had chosen her?

Tessa remembered these acts of bullying years later when she worked with colleagues who, for no reason that she could see, began to harass or set traps for her. Whenever this happened, the old Trinidadian proverb, "all grin teeth is not laugh" would come to her mind. And she was constantly surprised when people she had considered her friends stabbed her in the back or betrayed her to those in authority. She wondered whether she would ever be free of victimization, or whether there was something about her that encouraged such abuse. Did she wear a banner saying "Victim"?

And why was it that some people were always on the receiving end and others always the abusers? Her mother believed that such acts of aggression were rooted in jealousy, and were carried out by people hating to see others succeed. But Tessa was to find that workplace politics were subtler than this. And she was also to discover that defending the rights of the underdog was a dangerous thing, especially when one is also an underdog.

7.

"Split Me in Two"

S AN JUAN DE LA PINA, originally known as "Coolie Town," once had a prosperous sugar-cane estate in Peru village. It was written about by a famous writer, Lafcadio Hearn, who had gone searching for East Indian jewellery made by local artisans who were formerly indentured East Indians. The writer extolled the beauty of the East Indian women and children living in the dusty village in 1880.

San Juan de la Pina in the 1950s was now a vastly advanced suburb of the city of Port of Spain. Tessa often wondered why the district was called San Juan de la Pina, for there were no Spanish people living there that she knew of, and no pine trees that she could see. The population of the area was almost completely split between Blacks and East Indians. There were a few people of the more superior race—Chinese, Portuguese, poor whites, and mulattoes—most of whom lived on the Silk Cotton Road in modest-sized houses adorned with picket fences and gingerbread fronts of old-fashioned charm. The name Coolie Town had long been changed to San Juan de la Pina. Later, after Trinidad gained its independence from Britain, the first Prime Minister would outlaw the terms "*coolie*" and "*nigger*," words with which these two main population groups had be- rated each other for generations. The islanders had developed their own vocabulary, coining names for mixed-race Black and white people, names like *shabine, red nigger, red-skinned, light brown, or high brown.* And for anyone of mixed East Indian and Black blood, the term *dougla* was used. Tessa's brother Clyde was close friends with one such boy, Manny, who was a classmate and a frequent visitor to the Joseph household.

One evening when Manny was visiting, Tessa was surprised to hear the adults, for the first time, speaking frankly to an outsider on the touchy subject of race. Lucille Joseph and her sisters had grown up in a mixed-race village and had become friends with people of all races. The village of de Gannes, which lay on the outskirts of the city of Port of Spain, was unique in many respects. In the village, there had been families of Portuguese descent, Black and brown immigrants from Barbados and Tamil East Indians. The Samnaddan-Pillais knew that, in an emergency, their neighbours of every race would come to their aid; they were all struggling to keep body and soul together, or trying desperately to rise above their poverty. The Joseph family, now living in San Juan de la Pina, continued the tradition of respecting people of all races, never using the "N" word, and never putting down people because of their race. Since Manny was visiting, the whole family was sitting in the drawing room. Tessa and Sylvia were never excluded from conversations when visitors came, except when the aunts had some confidence to disclose or gossip to share. The ladies would then lock themselves in Lucille's bedroom or send the girls outside to play.

Lucille had brought out plates of her delicious coconut bread—called sweet bread, a favourite delicacy of the islanders—and glasses of orange juice, the usual refreshment offered to visitors, for it was inexpensive and always available in the house.

Manny had a narrow straight nose and the deep black eyes of his mother's East Indian heritage. His hair showed his Black blood. It was heavily greased, as was the prevailing fashion. Manny was tall and well built. Like so many young men of that time, he lifted weights to look like Charles Atlas. He was a boy filled with ambition and determination to succeed in life, and this made him rather morose.

"You went to say goodbye to your grandparents yet?" Lucille asked Manny.

"I don't want to go and see them. After how they treat my mother and how they hate my father, I don't see why I should go." Manny's eyes flashed with anger. He sounded harsh, a change from his usually mild tone.

Lucille countered, "But they are still your grandparents. As Christians, we must forgive others. I'm sure you learned that from the priests at school."

"But you know what? I only met my mother's family twice—once in their stall at the market, and another time when my mother went back to the village when her sister died and she took me with her." Manny was showing a firmness that none of them had ever seen in him before.

"Nobody was very friendly to us, except one cousin. I suppose it's because she is a teacher that she didn't have any prejudice towards Black people like most of the relatives. The rest of them are not very ambitious. They don't send their children to high school, and they don't seem to care much for education. Their girls are married at sixteen and seventeen, and have lots of children very soon. The boys are all working at semi-skilled jobs. I'm glad my father is an educated man and made me want to better myself."

Was Manny saying that the Indians were less progressive than the Black people? Tessa knew that since she was the youngest present, she couldn't challenge him on that. Her mother would only tell her to be quiet and stop asking questions.

"I still think you should go," Lucille Joseph said, trying to coax Manny into seeing things her way. "It will be a blessing before you leave for Canada to take up your scholarship."

"What blessing? They hate me and can't forgive my mother for marrying a Black man. I only knew my grandparents on my father's side; it was like I never had any others. I never got to know my cousins on my mother's side because they had cut us off."

"I think Manny is right," Clyde put in, "Why, you yourself always saying how we don't go to see our grandmother because she was not nice to us."

Their mother didn't say anything else. Tessa thought about how, because her mother's parents had long passed away, the children knew only their father's mother, Shakuntala, with whom her mother was not on friendly terms. They went to visit their grandmother only once a year, when she held her *pujas,* the Hindu prayers for beggars and the destitute. Lucille Joseph had never told the children what had caused the deep rift between herself and her mother-in-law. Once, when Tessa was eavesdropping, she heard her mother and her Aunt Marie reminiscing about the day that they had gone to Shakuntala's house to discuss Marie's wedding plans. Lucille and Marie had married two brothers.

"I don't think I will ever forget that day, even though it was you she insulted and not me," Lucille had said. "She couldn't really do anything to me. I was already married to her son. But she didn't want to see another son go. I think she would have kept them all at her house, if she could. She didn't want any of them to marry." Lucille's tone was one of disgust, one that Tessa had often heard her use when she was discussing anything that was distasteful to her, or any behaviour that she classified as low class or ugly.

"She didn't have to throw water on us," Aunt Marie had replied. "If she didn't want us coming into her house, that was no way to tell us. Our mother always said that Shakuntala comes from one of the lowest castes in India—that is why she behaves like that."

Tessa did not hear the word "caste" used very often. But occasionally, when Lucille was exasperated by behaviour she found despicable, she would revert to the demarcation of caste.

The wedding had gone on without Shakuntala. But it was only later that Tessa came to understand that there was something much graver between her mother and her grandmother than Shakuntala's "ignorant and low-caste behaviour," a deep injustice that Shakuntala had inflicted on Lucille that could never be repaired.

So why was her mother urging Manny to visit grandparents who had not wanted to see him or his mother for so many years? Tessa had heard the story of how they had thrown his mother out of the house when they found out she was pregnant. Not only pregnant, but the father was a Black man too. It was Manny's father's parents, Jack and Sadie ,who had taken in Manny's mother, Gemma, and arranged for her marriage to their son.

Tessa thought the reason her mother was urging Manny to visit his grandmother was because Lucille and all the aunts never liked to be on bad terms with anyone. Lucille and her sisters encouraged their children to do the same. Even when they were bullied on the playground or in the classroom, their mothers wouldn't go to the teachers and complain. Were they afraid to come to the school? Or did they just want to keep the peace?

"You hear the calypso on the radio by the calypsonian Dougla?" Manny asked, feeling that he had enough of the subject of his grandparents. No one in the house had heard it yet, but Manny sang the chorus. The song was about a *dougla,* like Manny, and the chorus was, "If they send the Africans back to Africa and the Indians back to India, what they will do with me? They will have to split me in two."

Everyone laughed.

"I sure hope The Mighty Dougla win the Calypso King Contest this year," said Clyde. "That calypso is telling a truth people don't understand. Because all of us have nowhere else to go, so must stay in this little island. And, we all come from someplace else, starting with the Spaniards who killed off the Aboriginals by putting them in reserves and working them to death. Some of the Indians poisoned the Capuchin Monks, while some others threw themselves off a cliff rather than be enslaved any more. The Spanish allowed French people to the island because they were Catholic too. And when slavery was finished, the British and French plantation owners brought indentured workers from Portugal, China, and India, because the white planters couldn't do the work in the hot sun."

"And the Portuguese and Chinese couldn't stand the hard work in the fields either, so they went off and opened shops and businesses. But what I don't understand is why the half-white people, the ones we call 'red-skin,' believe they better than us?" Manny asked. "They have white skin but they have Black blood in them too, like me. And they have curly hair like mine."

"Well, that," said Clyde, "is because many white plantation owners had children with their Black slaves, and then they brought these children in from the fields into the house and educated them. This is why the 'red-skin' people always lording it over people like us. They had a head start over us Indians who came after them. But then the Syrians came, selling cloth. First, they carried the cloth in bundles on their heads, and later in suitcases, and very soon they move on to buy stores in Port of Spain, and now they richer than everybody else; they even have more money and business than the old English and French creole families. And now every race in this little island looking down on every other, instead of trying to get along when we all have to live in this little thirty-seven-by-fifty-mile island."

Clyde knew all this from his West Indian reader history classes but also because he was a tireless reader of sociology, politics, and anthropology, and he always had information on all these topics at his fingertips.

Lucille added to Clyde's diatribe, saying that she believed the people from Africa and India, should get along peaceably because they needed each other. They were both oppressed by the other racial groups on the island and were at the bottom of the barrel, she added. Tessa was surprised when her mother said this, for in the past she had heard Lucille and her sisters discussing suitable marriage partners for their children, and she knew that they did not approve of anyone in the family marrying a Black person. Adults have their own rules about everything, Tessa reflected. And they were so confusing.

8.
Goberdhan Visit

L UCILLE AND HER FAMILY were visiting her niece Helena and her husband Sonny, who lived in a small village in the central part of the island. It was an annual visit, which entailed a long journey by pirate taxi from the city. Helena and Sonny lived with Sonny's widowed father, Kumar Goberdhan.

Helena and Kumar sat with their guests in the large open space underneath the two-storey house built on stilts. Weddings, funerals, and *pujas* were always held here in the country houses. The concrete floor was painted in a bright yellow, and it was clean and well-swept. They sat in wide rattan basket chairs covered with soft cushions of a bright floral pattern. Helena served tall glasses of the soft drinks the islanders called "sweet drinks." The locally made soft drinks were a recent innovation of the enterprising businessman Joseph Charles, who had bought a soft drink factory that was closing down. He had soon improved the product and expanded the business, eventually making a fortune by introducing local flavours such as banana, pineapple, and sorrel. The drinks were called Solo because Charles—who had started his business at home and with the help of his wife, mixed the drinks by hand—soon found he could not obtain an adequate supply of bottles from the island. He began to buy bottles from a Canadian soft drink factory that was going out of business, and since he had been unable to remove the labels, he kept the name. The drinks were now part of the island's rich storehouse of food and drink. People no longer had to go through the long process of making homemade drinks such as *mauby*, from the bark of a local tree, ginger beer from the pungent ginger, a root vegetable valued all over the world for its taste and medicinal qualities, or sorrel, the bright red fruit of a local plant. Making these drinks had been a time-consuming, arduous process. Thanks to Joseph Charles, the islanders now had, in addition to Pepsi and Coca-Cola, their own local soft drinks. They discovered that the red sorrel flavour blended perfectly with the hot curry rotis, which had become an island staple.

Helena had taken Sylvia with her to help serve the drinks. Since few people had fridges, a hand-held ice pick was used to chip pieces from a large block of ice obtained from the corner shop, and pieces of ice were put into every glass before serving the drinks. To serve drinks without ice in such a hot climate was considered an insult.

Tessa marvelled at the cool and peaceful surroundings, the silence broken only by the whistling birds fluttering from tree to tree. The black-and-yellow birds known as the *keskidee*, filled the air with its unique cry. According to local folklore, the French colonists, on hearing the shrill cry of the bird, thought it was asking, "*Q'est qu'il dit?*" This myth was handed down to the younger generation by teachers and elders.

Kumar Goberdhan, a small, thin, wiry man who wore rimless glasses that made him look like Mahatma Gandhi, was about seventy years old and one of the most prosperous men in the village. After some years of working on his father's land, Kumar had obtained a job in Port of Spain in a large department store, where he had to dress every day in dark slacks and a dress shirt and tie. Because the pay was paltry, he and his wife continued to cultivate vegetables. The rich tropical soil, always well watered from the copious rainfall the island enjoyed, nurtured many varieties of vegetables. Beans and peas, tomatoes, cucumbers, *patchoi*, zucchini—called by its French name *gouge*—and ground provisions such as cassava, yams, *dasheen, eddoes, khus-khus* and sweet potatoes, would all be found in the neighbourhood market. While this market garden supplemented their income, Kumar had ventured into various businesses—taxi driving and later truck driving—and eventually came to own a fleet of trucks. Now he had one of the largest houses in the village, and his neighbours, trying to keep up with him, soon converted their huts of mud and dung to concrete houses.

Kumar Goberdhan had managed to send his children not only to high school but also to university in Canada. His eldest son, nicknamed Sonny, had however always been involved in his father's enterprises and had finished high school. It was said that Sonny was so sullen and unfriendly because he felt that he was the one who had enabled his six brothers and three sisters to become doctors, lawyers, teachers, and school principals, while he tended the rum shop. Sonny would never be at the house whenever the Joseph family came to visit. Normally, he remained in his rum shop, even on Sundays, so it was a surprise when this Sunday he suddenly appeared and sat with them. He seldom had anything to say to the children. Or to the adults for that matter. Tessa remembered being taken to the rum shop on earlier visits, because Sonny had not come to the house to visit with them. She had been puzzled by the sign in the shop that read: *Opening and Closing Hours: Any day, any time.* She had passed by the rum shops on Main Road in San Juan de la Pina, and their signs had read: *Opening and Closing hours: 9:00 a.m to 9:00 p.m Monday to Thursday and 9:00 a.m. to 12:00 p.m. midnight on Friday and Saturday.* Why did the village rum shop have such a sign?

She had asked Clyde about it. "I don't know," he'd said. "Except perhaps if they state certain hours and they close earlier because business is slow, then their customers could complain and bang on their doors and get on, referring to the sign. I could just hear them saying, 'All yuh say de shop open till ten at night and is only eight o'clock and you shut down already.'

These village people take their rum-drinking serious, serious."

Tessa knew what Clyde meant by "getting on." It was making a scene, shouting and cussing and "carrying on," screaming loudly until they had their way.

Sonny was a tall and broad-shouldered man with a pot belly, the opposite, Tessa thought, of his slim and petite wife. Lucille always tried to engage him in conversation.

"So, the rum shop doing well, Sonny?" she asked.

"Is okay, is okay," he replied and squirmed in his chair.

Then Sonny tried to talk to Clyde. Tessa noticed how rough his voice was and how his sentences came and went in sudden spurts. She was embarrassed that this grown man was so un-comfortable trying to carry on a conversation with children.

"How the studies going, Clyde? You at Lourdes College, eh? What you going to do with all that book learning? Doctor or engineer or what?"

Clyde, Tessa knew, had no inclination to do either, for he hated science and often skipped classes to read heavy books about history, and politics, and even obscure subjects like an-thropology and palaeontology at the Central Library. Though his mother knew of these jaunts, she did not forbid them, for she indulged her only son to the chagrin of the two girls, who felt that he should not be allowed to skip school. The priests never enquired about these absences, either, for high school was not compulsory, and if their students did not care to acquire an education, it was not their problem. As long as the fees of sixteen dollars a term were paid, they had no more responsibility.

Clyde's answer to Sonny's enquiry was a laconic one.

"One of them, I guess. Or maybe law, I think."

"Well," Sonny said to Clyde, "better make sure you study your head good, and come out on top of your class. Me, I never went to high school. Only my brothers and sisters had the chance. I was working with my father and mother since I was nine years old."

The children felt sorry for him. They had heard this before, and that so much of the Goberdhans' wealth had been acquired through Sonny's ability and hard work. At nine years old, he had run the family's rice mill. At that early age, he arranged to sell the husks of the milled rice to the monks as feed for their animals. The monks of the Abbey ran a large, farming operation, rearing animals, growing crops and keeping honey bees, all of which enabled them to be self-sufficient. The monks had ibeen astute in selecting land on a high peak in the northern range with a breathtaking vista of the valley below. These Dutch priests had originally settled in Brazil, but, fearing negative repercussions from a changing political climate, they relocated to the island. The Abbey became a source of solace for people of many faiths. From his early commercial dealings with the monks, Sonny had gone on to develop other businesses, all successful. Clyde had remarked that it looked as if Sonny had the Midas touch, an allusion that he had to explain to Tessa. Why he was happy to remain running a rum shop now was a question that Lucille had often puzzled over, out loud, within the children's hearing.

Lucille had also voiced to her sisters her disapproval of her sister's decision to marry off her smart, pretty daughter to Sonny. Lucille thought her sister Althea had wronged Helena greatly by marrying her off to someone like Sonny, especially because she then had to live so far away from the rest of the familly. Tessa overheard her Aunt Clarissa say that Helena's parents, Althea and Mark, had been "approached" by Sonny's parents to ask whether they would consider Helena a suitable match for their son. Because of the Goberdhans' comfortable position, Helena's parents had agreed, especially because a serious illness had forced Helena's father to stop driving his taxi, which had been the family's only source of income. Even though Althea had started to take in washing from the neighbours, their life was still hard. The parents felt this offer of marriage was a heaven-sent opportunity. Helena was the eldest of four girls and with her husband now ill, there was no money to educate them. With Helena married, things would be a little easier. Lucille had said that it was a pity that Helena, a convent-educated girl, had to live day in and day out with such an uneducated and unrefined man as Sonny.

"Why didn't they match her up with one of the boys studying away, I wonder?" Tessa overheard her Aunt Clarissa saying to her mother one afternoon when she was eavesdropping as usual.

"Well, once the boys go away, they not going to come back for any arranged marriage," countered Lucille. "They will get hooked up with white women over there. And those women often glad to marry a doctor or engineer, even though he not white. But I hear that these girls in North America and England often help out the boys with money and food and introduce them to their families, and with the boys so lonely up there, they end up marrying them."

Aunt Clarissa had continued, "You wouldn't believe what a terrible life that poor girl had when she first went there to live. They lived in a dirt house at that time; they hadn't yet built the big house. And they had no inside toilet. Imagine that. None of our sisters ever had to bring up their children with outside toilets. Helena was walking around barefoot when I went to see her. And the mother-in-law was bullying her. Helena had to work in the rum shop, and then come home and cook and wash. The old lady didn't do anything. She was always complaining of some illness or other. You remember our mother with all those children, ever lying down sick? If she woke up in the morning not feeling too well, she would still get up, eat an orange, and be back on her feet again, doing her work."

"I never visited them in the old house. I think that was the time I had my trouble—Jeffrey's passing and my in-laws supposedly trying to help me, but instead, making things worse. Helena got lucky when the old lady didn't live too long after. What I heard about that man, Sonny, is that he is a real Mama's boy and didn't do anything to protect his wife from his mother.

The old Indian mother-in-law tradition. Where the daughter-in-law is to be treated like dirt. We were lucky we didn't have to live with mothers-in-law. Though I didn't live with mine, she still believed in the Indian tradition that an Indian widow is nothing. And so she made my life hell."

Tessa had overheard this conversation, and she thought she understood what had happened between her grandmother Shakuntala and her mother. However, she was not to learn the full truth about Shakuntala's behaviour and how it had affected her mother's life until years later.

Helena, who had gone upstairs to see to lunch, taking Sylvia to help her, came downstairs to tell them it was time to eat.

"You eating with us today, Sonny?" she asked her husband in her quiet voice. Tessa thought Helena sounded as if she was begging him to do so.

"No, not today. I have to get back to the rum shop now. I will see you all later."

He didn't even say, "No, sorry, I can't stay," Tessa thought. And why did he even bother to say "not today"? He had never once stayed and had lunch with them in all the years they had been coming here.

Soon, from the dusty lane that lay adjacent to the house, they saw a white man, a rarity in these East Indian villages, approaching the house. He entered the yard and came up to Kumar. He was dressed in a black suit with the white collar of a preacher.

"Good afternoon, Mr. Goberdhan." He greeted Kumar politely, removed his hat, bowed to Lucille, and Helena and said, "Hello children." He had the drawl of the American southerner.

"Yes?" Kumar Goberdhan addressed the preacher. "How you know I am Goberdhan?"

"Well, the people in the village directed me here. My name is Pastor Ryan Smith. They said you had a large house with an unused space underneath, and I am looking for such a place."

"Why?" asked Goberdhan. His tone was curt, and Tessa

thought that the American man was sure to get scared and leave quickly without stating his business. "What you want it for?"

"Well, you can see I am a preacher. And I hope to start a Sunday School for the children. Yours is the only house without a rum shop or parlour or some business underneath. I would be very happy if you could let me use here every Sunday for the children, to teach them about God."

Kumar Goberdhan thought this over for a minute. He had not become prosperous by making impulsive decisions. "What time so you will have this Sunday School?" he asked.

"Every Sunday afternoon at two o'clock. By that time lunch would be long over. I know how everyone here has a big Sunday lunch."

"Well." Kumar did not want to appear anxious to give an answer. After a while he asked his daughter-in-law, "What you think Helen? You think it's all right for me to allow this man, this stranger, to hold a Sunday School here?"

Helena, like a good Indian daughter-in-law, bent her head and said, "Bap, is up to you. Is your house, after all. But I don't see anything wrong if you say yes."

Kumar finally said to the preacher, "I suppose it should be all right. You are a man of God, and I can't see what harm there would be in letting you have the place for a few hours every week."

The preacher could hardly contain his gratitude and relief. "God will shower wealth and blessings on you and your family, I am sure of it," he proclaimed in a prophetic voice. Then, more subdued, he asked, "Would it be alright if we started next Sunday? I have the children already. I only needed a place."

"Yes, yes, yes," Goberdhan assured him, waving his hand. Having made his decision, he did not care to discuss it further. "We will see you next week then."

Pastor Smith replaced his hat on his bald head, shook Goberdhan's hand, and even Lucille's and Helena's, beamed at the children, and practically skipped out of the yard.

After their Sunday lunch, a typical Indian lunch of *roti*, *dahl*, and curried chicken with a dish of highly seasoned fried eggplant, tomato, and onions, called *melongene chokkha*, they were all sitting downstairs again when they saw the pundit, the Hindu priest, approaching. The children were interested. It was the first time they had met so many visitors at their cousin's house, and a pundit was a treat. They were used to seeing the Imams, the Moslem priests—San Juan de la Pina had many more Moslems than Hindus. The suburb had a Moslem mosque, a beautiful white structure, but no Hindu Temple. The *pundit* was dressed all in white in a *dhoti* and a long shirt called a *kurta* that reached just above his knees. He wore a saffron turban called a *pugaree* on his head and a string of holy beads around his neck. He was a thin, nervous-looking man whose brow was furrowed into a permanent frown, and he did not look happy. Tessa wondered if the many intricate rituals he had to perform weighed him down.

She had seen some of these rituals when her grandmother had her *pujas*, which she called "dinners" and at which she fed the poor and destitute. The poor were fed downstairs, and the ceremony on the second floor of the two-storey house was only for the family and neighbours who wished to take part. During the ceremony, the pundit sat on the ground, which was covered with a spotlessly clean white sheet. A large box served as the altar and held pictures of three gods, Hanuman, Lakshmi, and Vishnu. Each god's picture was flanked by its own flag—red for Hanuman, pink for Lakshmi, and white for Vishnu—each on a small bamboo stick.

Freshly picked flowers—red ixora, red as well as orange hibiscus, buttercups of white and yellow, white oleander, and marigold, and leaves of the mango tree—were scattered on the table underneath the pictures of the gods. The gods' pictures were adorned with garlands made of hibiscus flowers. In the middle of the altar was a small round clay pot called a *deya*. This was filled with oil and a cotton wick and was lit.

At the front of the altar was a tub with the branch of a young banana tree surrounded with offerings of oil, camphor, incense, and fruit in brass dishes. As they sat on the floor on the clean white sheets and watched the pundit do the various rituals, wash the fruit, and make several offerings, they listened to the incantations in Tamil and inhaled the scents of the burning camphor and incense. Tessa marvelled at the whole ceremony, so different from Easter and Christmas celebrations at church. And yet there were many similarities, she thought. A priest, chanting, the use of incense and flowers, and the ringing of small bells. They did not blow a conch shell in church, but they had singing and organ music. The ceremony was very long, and often the children got restless and had to be taken out of the prayer room.

After the ceremonies, the family and visitors sat downstairs on folding chairs brought in for the occasion. All the neighbours from the village would come to the *puja*. One woman stood out from the others, for her style of dress was unique. She wore the costume of the women of the French Caribbean island of Martinique. Tessa had seen this costume at Carnival, and on every Saturday morning when a woman dressed like this came from the hills to their house on Victory Street. She carried a basket on her head laden with vegetables and French pastries. She addressed Lucille as *Macomere,* and she spoke broken English, for French Patois was her native tongue. This woman who attended her grandmother's *pujas* was dressed in the same style and, strangest of all, smoked a pipe. Tessa was fascinated by this woman. She knew that her own great-grandmother had come as a six-year-old child with her father from Martinique. However, her great-grandmother, Pauline, had not retained her Martiniquan dress and had become an entrepreneur, running a small village shop. When Tessa knew her, she was bedridden in a small room in the house of one of her granddaughters, a room which reeked of Bay Rum and Tiger Balm. But it was clear from her very white skin that her mother must have been a French woman. Why this child was brought by her Indian father alone, without any wife, was never explained. Perhaps he been banished by the French plantation owners in Martinique because he had fathered a child with one of their daughters. Or had his wife passed away? No one really knew.

Tessa's visits to the "dinners," or *pujas*, were always spoiled when her grandmother introduced her to the adults by saying, "This is my first son's last child. This is the one who was in the mother belly when he dead." The murmurings of sympathy were not enough to make up for Tessa's embarrassment at her grandmother's way of saying that Tessa had been born three months after her father's passing. Tessa knew that her mother never said "belly" or that a woman was "making baby" like the common people did. Instead she would say "tummy" or that a woman was "having a baby." And Lucille did not speak broken English like her mother-in-law, Shakuntala. She would not have said "when he dead," but "when he passed away." But what bothered Tessa most was that she was made to feel that she had committed a crime in being born after her father's death. It was as if she were illegitimate, which everyone knew was a blot on a person's character. To have "illegitimate" scrawled across your birth certificate would prevent you from getting into the best schools, or getting good jobs; it was a handicap that followed you the rest of your life. Yet, Tessa soon realized that such rules did not apply to anyone who had money. The man they called Uncle Simon, one of her father's business partners, had a second family with an "outside" woman and the children, who were all illegitimate, attended the best convent school. Lucille's comment on this was, "You see? You can get anywhere in this place as long as you have money."

"Kumar?" the pundit addressed Mr. Goberdhan. "I have something I want to talk over with you."

"Sit down, sit down, Pundit Narine. As you see, my daughter-in-law has some family visiting from the city."

Introductions were made, and the pundit seated himself. He

seemed uncomfortable, as though he wanted to talk privately with Goberdhan. But since this looked like it would be difficult without awkwardness, he decided to speak. "Kumar, the people in the village tell me that you going to let the white preacher man from the United States run a Sunday school here, under your house."

"Yes, that is true. But how you hear that so soon? You wasn't drinking in my son's rum shop? Is only there all the gossip does travel fast, fast." Kumar had a twinkle in his eye.

"No, no, I don't go to the rum shop. But I meet my son-in-law, that boy always there. He was coming out of the shop and he tell me what he hear about the Sunday school you going to allow under your house."

"Well? Is that something wrong that I will be doing?"

Goberdhan leaned back in his deep basket chair and spoke in a tone that would not be easy to oppose. He was his own man, and once he had made a decision, he wasn't going to let anyone, even a pundit, tell him it was a bad one.

"But, Kumar, I don't understand how you, a practising Hindu, can allow this man to come and preach in your house to all these Hindu children. This is a wrong thing you doing, Goberdhan."

The pundit shook his head from side to side to emphasize his point. "Why we letting this man with his foreign religion corrupt us from our own eastern Hinduism? Christianity is not our religion. Is the white man own. It will change our children. I warning you, Goberdhan."

His voice was rising with every word he uttered, and he took out his handkerchief from the folds of his *dhoti* and wiped his brow.

Kumar Goberdhan replied, "To show that our *dharma* is greater, we have to be accepting of other religions and treat people of other faiths with kindness and respect. But besides that, I want to ask you something, Pundit. You think the preacher will teach the children to do wrong things or right things?"

Pundit Narine was silenced and took his leave, somewhat curtly.

As sour and unfriendly as Sonny Goberdhan was, his old father was the opposite. He and Helena, who got along well, were united in wicked glee at the pundit's discomfort.

Helena said, "Bap, you know what I hear about that pundit? He was doing a *puja* for the Sunderban family, and in addition to all the things they had to buy—the camphor and oil and the ingredients to make all the food and the sweets—he said they had to give him a bed. A bed! Nobody ever hear anything like that before."

Hindu *pujas* were as elaborate as any formal western-style dinner, and they cost money. There was *roti*, rice, curried pumpkin, sweet and hot chutney of mango and *pommecythere*. There were fried savoury snacks of *phoulorie* and *saheena*, and many sweets such as *kurma*, *rasgoolas* and *gulab jamun*. And the holy offering known as *prasad*, which was made of flour sugar and raisins, must also be accompanied by fruit. It was also the custom for all the guests to be sent home with a parcel of food. *Pujas* were not cheap. So to ask for a bed in addition to his fee and all the expenses of the food was dishonest and inconsiderate, they thought.

Kumar, on hearing the story of the pundit, launched into a tale about the pundit of his childhood. He had been sent by his mother to take a large quantity of rice to the pundit as an offering for having performed a *puja*. These *pujas* were usually held in homes after momentous events like births and deaths. On returning home, after delivering the rice to the pundit, Kumar said to his mother, "Ma, you think it right that we, who so poor, and work so hard to plant this rice have to give away all this to the pundit, who so much richer than we? He living in a big two-storey concrete house, and we in this mud hut."

Though his mother and father had scolded him for question-ing their religion and their judgement, later that night he had overheard his parents laughing at his observation, saying that the child was right, for he had put into words a truth they had often considered themselves.

Helena laughed and said, "I think all religions the same, Aunt Lucille. You remember what happened to our cousin, Jennifer? When she went to become a nun she was supposed to give a dowry to the convent. But if she got married in the Catholic church, her parents wouldn't have to give a dowry like the Hindu people have to do. So why she had to give a dowry to the church when the family was so poor, I could never understand. And in the end, she didn't stay. When she came out, she was a wreck. Nobody knew what happened to her in the convent. She doesn't talk about it."

Lucille sighed. "Yes, I know. I thought my sister Joanie was wrong to allow Jennifer, a seventeen-year-old girl to go and join the convent. I don't think seventeen is old enough to know what you want in life."

Tessa was surprised to hear her mother criticize her sister for allowing Jennifer to join the convent. Tessa remembered how the aunts had made such a fuss when Jennifer had been accepted into the order of the Sisters of the Good Shepherd. It was an honour, the aunts and her mother had said. An honour for Jennifer. And for the family, of course. The church represented the ruling class, and by being a nun or priest you automatically rose higher up on the social scale. Tessa was not to understand this until years later—after Independence, after her years of study, after the whites no longer held all the power in the island.

Tessa was impressed with Kumar Goberdhan. She and Clyde talked about him as they walked to the main road to flag down a taxi to take them home.

The Main Road was a welter of cars, bicycles, animals, and people, all fighting for supremacy on the narrow street. The sidewalks were crammed with vendors' stalls offering everything from food, shoes, dresses, pots and pans, to women's bras and panties on full display. Walking was a test of agility, as the stalls occupied most of the sidewalk, which was broken in places and deliberately cut in others to accommodate driveways. Mangy, half-starved dogs roamed through the crowds or were sprawled out in a sound sleep on every corner. The Joseph family had to manoeuvre through animal excrement on the sidewalk, and now and then they had to avoid a vagrant lying prone and senseless in their path.

"O gad," said Sylvia. "San Juan de la Pina is not like this. What kind of streets and pavements they have in the country?"

"What pavements? You can't see how they block up the pavements with stalls?" said Clyde.

"The people here don't know any better. They think this is how a main road should be. How many of them ever go to town to see how other people live?" This was Lucille, who was always glad that she lived in town, and not "in the country."

"Boy, that Kumar Goberdhan is something, I tell you. Imagine him talking to the pundit like that," said Clyde.

"That is because he have common sense and not education sense," their mother was quick to reply.

Lucille believed that some people could become stupid with too much education. That did not include her children, who were encouraged to get as much education as they could stomach or "take," as the islanders said. She disdained the new subject of psychology, seeing it as a front for other evils.

"But would you talk to your priest like that?" asked Tessa, challenging her mother, who accepted everything the church said without question. "What if you were in Uncle Kumar's shoes, and the priest told you not to let an Adventist minister or whatever he is, have a Sunday School under your house? I bet you would never dare to disobey him."

"Well...." Lucille was not sure what she would do if she were in Goberdhan's shoes, so she dismissed the question airily with, "I don't have any big upstairs house with room underneath, so I don't have to worry."

Clyde looked at Tessa and Sylvia. The two girls and their brother exchanged smiles. They had often talked among themselves about their mother's tendency to skirt around problems, refusing to face them if they were too difficult. Her answer was proof of this. Tessa, led by the two older ones, was beginning to see this flaw in her mother and to question all the rules of living that her mother and the adults around her advocated. And there were so many, Tessa reflected.

9.
Wider Horizons

SYLVIA AND TESSA, now thirteen and eleven years old, were at San Juan de la Pina school with their mother. It was Saturday morning, and Sister Bernadette, the principal, had requested a visit with Mrs. Joseph.

Sister Bernadette was a short, pink-faced white woman, and she had transformed the poor primary school into one of the best in the city of Port of Spain. She and Mrs. Labadie, the fourth standard teacher, had enrolled the children under twelve to take the annual College Exhibition Exam, something that the school had never done before. Children who earned places in the first hundred would then have free secondary education at the top schools for the next five years. Otherwise, parents would have to pay the fees for their children to acquire a high school education. A number of "private" secondary schools had sprung up, run by enterprising men who saw the need not only for high schools on the island but also for a chance to make good money. These schools were purely utilitarian in their educational practices; they had no grounds for cricket or soccer, and their teachers were often only one grade above their students in education. Anyone emerging from these schools with a second or first grade in the Cambridge Senior School Certificate examination would have done so by sheer brain and will power. Many students had to attend these schools, often because their elementary schools had not prepared them adequately for the College Exhibition or the entrance exams for the prestigious Grammar schools, called the Convents and Colleges. Ironically, the fees for these "private" schools were higher than those for the grammar schools.

Sister Bernadette came from the local white aristocracy and belonged to the Order of the Sacred Heart. The nuns of this order wore floor-length, white habits. Long rosaries with immense black beads, attached to their waists by long white girdles, hung from one side, falling almost to the hems of their habits. In close quarters, the nuns usually held on to their rosaries so that they would not knock against objects in their paths. Their wimples were tightly moulded to their heads and necks, and white veils hung down to their waists. Their long, flowing sleeves were loose about the wrists while underneath their arms were covered with a long-sleeved shirt buttoned at the wrist. An oversized black crucifix on a huge cord hung around their necks, over a circular piece that covered their habits from their shoulders to their waists. Sometimes, however, when the nuns raised their arms too high during some strenuous action, the children could see that there was a large triangular piece of white cloth like a huge bra flattening their breasts.

Sister Bernadette was a very dedicated principal and emphasized music as well as academics. The first song that Tessa learned was "Coming through the Rye." But the strange words, "gin a body" and "coming through the rye" were not explained to the children. What was "gin" and what was "rye?" If they had been singing about sugarcane or cocoa or coconuts it would have been a different matter. Another song they learned was "John Peel." It was a wild, rollicking song that Tessa loved about John Peel hunting with his hounds and his hare in the morning, but what in heaven's name was "D'ye ken?" No one explained those words either.

When they were being taught "Polly Wolly Doodle," Tessa noticed how the piano teacher, a Black woman, winced and was visibly shaken when the children sang the words, "*I jumped on a nigger and I thought he was a hoss.*" Tessa was embarrassed that they would have to sing such words when there were so many Black people in the school, in the neighbourhood, and in the church—in fact half the people on the island were Black, and using that word was an insult.

The school's choirs often placed second at the Music Festival because no school could beat the choirs of Sacred Heart Convent School. At San Juan de la Pina Catholic Girls' School, the students were taught good manners, how to sit and act like ladies, and how to read out loud and speak in public. They enunciated their words properly, putting their tongues between their teeth and pronouncing the "th's," instead of saying *dey* for *there* or *dem* for *them* as most islanders did. The children were taught how to use a measured tone when speaking instead of the sing-song intonations or the overly-loud voices that most people used. The teachers spoke with proper English accents, albeit with a Caribbean flavour, and by osmosis and constant correction as they read out loud, the children soon imitated them. Speaking with a good accent and proper grammar—not using "he" and "she" in the objective case or saying "come leh we go" instead of "come let us go"—set them apart from uneducated people, or people who did not go to the right schools. But above all, the students were submerged in the waters of the Roman Catholic faith. A large statue of the Blessed Virgin Mary perched on a white tablecloth fringed with lace, occupied a prominent place in the centre of the one room school. The school was the size of any small country church, about five hundred feet long and four hundred wide. The choir loft had been retained and it housed an additional class. The Virgin was dressed in a long white gown, her head was covered in a blue veil, and a blue girdle encircled her waist. Her arms were outstretched and her feet crushed a vile-looking serpent. A vigil light always burned at this altar.

Mrs. Joseph, Sylvia, and Tessa approached the principal's desk, which was on a high podium on the school stage and afforded a clear view of the entire room. Sister Bernadette, who sat in a large, high, stuffed chair, looked up from her book and indicated to the Joseph family that they should sit on three straight chairs that had been placed opposite to hers.

"What school are you planning to send the girls to?" Sister Bernadette asked.

Tessa knew her mother wouldn't have had the time to think about it. She had never brought up the subject with them. Tessa had never heard her mother talk about the future, for Lucille existed from day to day, always worrying about money and when she could afford to pay her grocery bill.

She shrugged her shoulders. She said to Sister Bernadette, "I haven't decided. Their cousins are going to the Meadowbrook Intermediate School. I thought perhaps I could send them there too."

"Sylvia can go to the Meadowbrook School. All you have to do is to go and see the nuns and register her there. It is too late for her to take the entrance exam for the Convent of the Sacred Heart—it's for those under twelve. But I think Tessa should take the exam," Sister Bernadette said firmly. "The exam will be held next Saturday. She will have to be at the convent at nine in the morning. Be sure that she is on time."

Mrs. Joseph agreed. But Tessa was worried. She knew that her brother's school fees for Our Lady of Lourdes College were being paid by one of her father's business partners, as there had been an agreement between the three men that if one should pass away, the others would ensure the sons of the late partners would be educated. There had been no mention of the girls' education.

As they walked home, Tessa said to Lucille, "Mum, how we will pay the fees for the convent if I pass the exam?" Everyone knew how high the fees for the convent were, while those for the Meadowbrook School were miniscule.

"Don't bother yourself about that," her mother said, patting Tessa on the shoulder. "You are too young to worry about big people's things. I will find the money. If other people, like Mrs.

Thomas and Mrs. Stevens who living in shacks by the ravine, and your Aunt Violet who living in a lil' wooden house behind her shop, could send their children to the convent, why I can't do that too?"

Tessa knew that Mrs. Thomas was a seamstress and Mrs. Stevens took in washing, and both had husbands; one worked on the wharf, while the other planted a vegetable garden in the hills above San Juan de la Pina. Her mother, however, was solely dependent on the monthly stipend she received after rescuing what was left of their money from the clutches of her in-laws, and it was not a big sum. Aunt Violet, a widow like her mother, supported herself and her four children with the income from a small corner shop which, though not as large and prosperous as Aunt Clarissa's, enabled her to pay the fees for her three boys to go to high school, and her only daughter, Camille, to go to the Sacred Heart Convent. She even sent Camille for piano lessons.

Those who took piano lessons seemed a cut above everyone else, for the island's culture was a musical one, and singing at the Music Festival and performing at piano recitals were very highly regarded. Tessa adored her cousin Camille, who had passed many music exams. Besides the classical music taught at the island schools, there was the music of the steel band and the brass bands that accompanied the revellers on Carnival days. At Tessa's house, the family enjoyed listening to the songs played every morning on Radio Trinidad, which included Latin American and world famous classical singers. They heard John McCormack, Jussi Bjorling, and later Mario Lanza, as well as the Latin craze of the United States, Xavier Cugat. One of the islanders had become successful in England, and his records were played frequently. This golden-voiced boy from San Juan de la Pina, Jan Mazurus, had appeared in the stage musical, *The King and I* in London.

On Friday nights on the radio show *Local Talent on Parade*, men with no musical training other than what they had received at their elementary schools would attempt to sing some of the songs made popular on the radio programs. Some would be surprisingly good, for they had been born with great voices and an ear for music. People would sit at their radios on Friday nights and hold their breaths wondering if the singer would "reach" the high notes or "bust" when they sang Gounod's "Ave Maria" or "The Holy City."

Camille sometimes came to visit after school. One afternoon she sat with the family in the drawing room, around the mahogany dining table, which was now used only for homework. Too often the children were interrupted from their assignments when visitors came to the front door of the small house and sat and chatted in the tiny drawing room. Tessa often thought that it would be nice to have a quiet room to herself in which to do her homework. But when it was Camille who was visiting, Tessa didn't mind; she was her favourite cousin. Camille was tall and slim and graceful, with a head of beautiful, thick, and curly black hair. She sang beautifully, and she was in the prestigious Sacred Heart Convent choir. She was only one of the two girls in the family attending the convent, but the other cousin, Priscilla, who also had a good singing voice, was not in the choir. The relatives thought it must be because Priscilla was painfully shy and hardly ever spoke.

Just as Clyde had predicted on the first night in the new house, the Joseph family could hear the mother from next door calling to her children in the back yard.

"Jacqueline and Ernest, come inside right now and bathe. Or else is cut-tail for you tonight."

"O, gom, Ma, Ernest still trying to get the mangoes at the top of the tree. Is only there it have ripe ones. Jus' now, na. You want Ernest to fall down if you hurry him up so?" Jacqueline pleaded with her mother.

"Yuh hear me? Right now, I say, not tomorrow or next year but now. All yuh father coming home just now. And you bound to get it if I tell him."

Everyone heard Jacqueline say, "Is all right, Ernest, you nearly reach that red mango up there, get it nuh man. If you don't pick it tonight, by tomorrow it would be smashed on the ground or it would have bird pick all over it." No one would eat bird-pecked mangoes, or those that had fallen from the great height and were all crushed and mushy.

Clyde looked out the drawing room window. But Ernest, a strapping eleven-year-old, scrambled down from the top of the Mango Vert tree. He wasn't risking a licking from his father, which could be long and violent.

Once things had quieted down, Camille told them about her plans to go to England to study music after her school leaving exams.

"It won't be easy to find the money. I'll have to work when I get there so I can study for more music exams. And sometimes I feel that I'm not getting enough training from Mrs. Delancey. Especially after the way she treats me when I go for lessons at her house."

"What you mean by the way she treats you when you go for lessons at her house?" Sylvia asked.

"I have to teach all the younger students, and then when it's quite late, nearly seven o'clock, and I would have been there since four, she will tell me to play my piece. Then she'll go into the kitchen to make her dinner. In between cutting up her vegetables and stirring her pot, she will call out to me if she hears me strike a wrong note."

"What?" Tessa was indignant on hearing this. Who this Mrs. Delancey think she is, to treat Camille like this? she thought. For Camille was talented in many other ways besides singing and playing the piano. She could sew dresses, knit, and do embroidery, as well as make layered tea sandwiches and exotic tea dainties the islanders called *bouchees*. Camille missed having a little sister, and when Tessa went to spend weekends with her, she curled Tessa's hair with strips of brown shop paper and taught her how to make rag mats from old cloth cut into strips. Aunt Violet, Camille's mother, lived behind her shop, an old wooden structure, in rooms which were small, dark, and poky, but Tessa loved going there because during the day the shop was a hive of activity. Camille and Tessa never served in the shop; Aunt Violet and the three boys did that. Whenever she and Camille had occasion to go into the shop, Tessa was intrigued by the wooden crates of salted cod and smoke herring, and the big shiny tins containing the salt butter. Customers would come and ask for "a penny salt butter" which was then was carefully ladled onto squares of brown paper. Tessa was fascinated by everything in the shop. The huge barrels of flour and sugar from which one and two-pound parcels could be scooped out and measured. And the barrels containing food the islanders had come to consider indispensable to their diet: pig's feet and pigtail in brine. With these parts of the pig, the enterprising island cooks had concocted many dishes. They made *souse,* slimy with sliced cucumbers and reeking of hot peppers and they used the pigtail to spice up their rice and peas dish that they called *pelau.* But though being behind the shop's counter instead of in front of it, and inhaling all the tantalizing aromas excited Tessa's sensibilities, it was really the way the customers respectfully addressed her aunt as "Miss Violet" that impressed Tessa.

But Tessa was soon to see those same people in a different light. It was the day when the government announced an end to the rationing of rice as the war was now over. When the shipment of rice arrived, the customers went crazy, shouting and pushing, crowding into the small shop, causing her Aunt Violet to faint. Were these the same nice polite people she had seen in the shop on other occasions? Tessa wondered. When she told her mother about it, Lucille said, "Imagine such behaviour! To carry on so, for a few grains of rice! To behave like animals! Those people have no breeding."

But remembering how hard her Aunt Violet worked in the small shop and how mean the people had been to her, Tessa was indignant at the story of Mrs. Delancey's treatment of Camille and said to her, "But why you don't tell your mother? Why you letting her do that to you? You paying good money for her to teach you. How people like her can get away with things like that, I just can't understand."

"You know how my mother is," Camille said, looking Lucille squarely in the eye. "And you too, Aunt Lucille. None of you sisters like to complain or make a fuss. You always afraid of people like Mrs. Delancey, high class Negroes as you call them. We poor Indian people don't know how to deal with them."

Lucille looked uncomfortable for a moment. She bent her head but she recovered quickly and replied, "We have to get along with everybody, of all races. And anyway, your mother don't want to quarrel with Mrs. Delancey. She will tell you not to come back to her piano school. Or she might behave worse. We all know she's the best piano teacher around. You have to put up with things like that, if you want to get any-where in life."

Tessa knew that Camille's criticism of their mothers was true. But Clyde, who was now sixteen years old, and whose head was filled with ideas about justice and equality and fighting back, lit into his mother vigorously.

"Why you let people take advantage of you all the time? Look at Aunt Eva. She let that woman come and stay in her yard, in the servant's quarters she had there, and now she can't get rid of her. She complaining to everybody, but can't put the woman out, even though she hasn't paid rent for the last six months. That must be your Hindu culture of passivity, that you can't let go of in this western world."

Once again Tessa found herself wondering why her mother always talked about getting along and not fighting back when-ever people treated them like this. She felt sick inside as she thought about how the Josephs and most of the people in their extended family were always being bullied by everyone else in the city. Perhaps one day when she, Sylvia, and Clyde were grown up, they would be so rich and important that nobody would push them around.

Thinking about all this, and feeling more and more unhappy, Tessa decided to pick up the newspaper. She was an avid reader and read the newspaper religiously every day. She came upon an article in which one of their cousin's wives was mentioned. Though she could read the words, she did not understand their significance.

"Listen to this," Tessa read out loud. "Mrs. Marilyn Soodeen was sent to jail for keeping a brothel."

"What?" Clyde exclaimed. "Let me see that," he said, taking the paper from her.

Camille and Lucille burst out laughing. Camille asked Tessa, "Do you know what a brothel is?"

"No, not really," Tessa had to admit, confused as to why everyone was laughing at her. She had only read what was in the paper.

"Oh, that Marilyn, Selwyn's wife, she's a bad woman. His father put him out of the house when he hear Selwyn was going around with her," sighed Lucille. "And now he went and marry her, and all she doing is blackening the Soodeen name. And how many people in Port of Spain have that name, I ask you? And everyone knows they related to us. For a relative of ours to be involved in that kind of bacchanal is a crying shame. The disgrace she bringing to this family." Lucille looked around the table at the young people. Then she turned to Clyde.

"Clyde, let this be a lesson to you. Watch out what kind of woman you get hook up with. You better make sure is not somebody like this Marilyn, this woman who come from we don't know what kind of family in Guyana. That country not like our little island, you know. She must be come from the bush, not from the city, and they always doing black magic that they learn from the Amerindians there. We call them *wharahoons*. Now this story in the paper for the whole island to see is a blot on the good name of our family."

Tessa knew Lucille was very fond of Selwyn. He had been an Island Scholarship runner-up, and everyone had expected him to become a doctor. When Selwyn's father had thrown him out of the house, Lucille had taken him in, and Selwyn had stayed at the Joseph's house for some weeks, sleeping on the floor in the drawing room. Lucille had not known what the quarrel was about. When the relationship with this Guyanese woman came to light, and Selwyn married her, everyone was scandalized, and Lucille humiliated. And now this. Of course, Lucille was upset.

As the adults talked, Tessa became more worried and confused. It had been drummed into them from their early years that family reputation was sacred. The aunts and relatives always felt personally humiliated when anyone in the large extended family disgraced them by doing anything illegal or against the laws of respectability they had set out for themselves. Keeping a brothel and being jailed for the crime amounted to "low-class" behaviour. It was not part of the culture of their family. She wondered whether her mother would continue to be nice to Selwyn, in spite of what his wife had done. Tessa made a silent vow to herself never to disgrace the family by doing anything scandalous. And she hoped that neither Clyde nor Sylvia would either. For keeping the good name of the family was something to be prized. To deviate from that path meant ostracism from the rest of the family.

10.

The Convent School

IN 1950, THE NEWS that Tessa had passed the Entrance Exam for the Convent of the Sacred Heart brought a spate of congratulations from relatives and neighbours. But to her consternation she also received so much advice about how hard she was expected to work that she began to feel that life would be unbearable for the next five years. In addition to the burden of maintaining the respectability of the family by keeping to the straight and narrow path, she was now handed another burden, that of being a model student, one who never shirked school work or behaved in a manner not befitting a "convent girl." Tessa was happy to find out that her best friend, Brenda, had also passed and would be in her class. This meant that they could travel to school and do their homework together.

Sylvia would go to the Meadowbrook Catholic Girls' School. This school had recently been taken over by an order of nuns newly arrived from Ireland. They were from the Order of the Good Shepherd. Unlike nuns of the Order of the Sacred Heart, the Good Shepherd nuns wore huge wimples that stuck out in front of their faces. The nuns had great ambitions for the school; they planned to elevate it into a fully-fledged convent grammar school, except for the lower fees. Every year the school's senior students presented an operetta, and the school had a Sea Scout troupe, which was like the Girl Guides, but focused on sea activities. Many of the school's students were able to pass their Senior Cambridge School Certificate exams, which earned them a ticket to a better life as civil servants, nurses, or teachers—which were the only careers that Blacks and East Indians could expect to secure.

Tessa was aware that the Convent of the Sacred Heart, for which she had passed the rigorous and highly competitive exam, was a prestigious school. Camille, who came over to congratulate her, told her about the school's long and glorious past. Founded in 1836, the school was originally for the girls of the British and French-Creole families of the island. In 1836, Black people were still slaves, and it was only after slavery was abolished that the East Indians came to the island in 1845. So the school was a whites-only school until the 1940s.

"Now there are some East Indians like me and Bhagwantia from Cocorico. But we are only a minority. Most of the students are still white or high-coloureds and high-brown mulattoes. And a few rich Chinese and Syrians, and some Black girls too. Of course, anyone who has earned a college exhibition scholarship has to be admitted, no matter what her colour or race. I hear you will be in the A stream," Camille said.

"What do they mean by 'stream?'" asked Tessa.

"The A stream students do Math, Latin, French, Spanish, and Biology, while the other streams concentrate on more practical subjects. Everyone, however, does Cookery, Needlework and Art for the first three years. You will learn your French from a nun who is from Paris; you have to call her Mère Jeanne," Camille continued, "and the Spanish nun has to be called Madre Magdalena. But you mustn't let her hear you using any Venezuelan expressions. She'll get mad, because she says she teaches Castilian Spanish, not Venezuelan Spanish."

"But where do all these nuns come from?" Tessa was puzzled. "I thought the nuns and priests all came from Ireland."

"Oh, the Sisters of the Sacred Heart have convents all over Europe, and the Mother House can move them wherever they are needed."

Tessa thought about how lucky her school was to have these nuns run a school for the island's children. After all, we're living in a backwater, she thought. It was a phrase she had heard Clyde use.

She knew she was privileged to be a part of this illustrious school. Attending the convent was a source of pride. But she soon realized that the school really belonged to the white upper-class girls, and the rest were merely tolerated.

In her first term, a handful of girls had not paid for the Needlework materials. "You are very careless girls," ranted Sister Marguerite, an old French nun, whose English was highly accented. Her face was lined and her back was bent, but her fingers were steady when she showed them how to work with the fine embroidery thread and needle.

"If we do not have the materials," she said, "how can I teach you to embroider fine pillowcases and tea towels? And little chemises for the babies?" Babies were always clothed in tiny cotton gowns that were finely smocked at the necklines, and smocking was considered an art.

The girls who were being scolded began to mutter at the nun under their breath. Angela Spence, who sat next to Tessa, and had also forgotten her needlework money said, "Who she think she talking to? The ole' cow so miserable, and she won't stop talking."

Angela Spence was one of the "difficult" girls who didn't have to worry about pleasing the nuns. Angela, though white-skinned—her father was white, her mother Black—had "pressed" hair; its natural thick curls had been straightened with a hot comb. Her father had an important job in Barclay's Bank, and he travelled extensively.

Because the nun was half deaf, she didn't hear any of it. At twelve years old, the girls considered sewing and embroidery something only their grandmothers did, and they were not interested in babies. What was the use of these classes? They shrugged and steupsed. Whether people in the rest of the world steupse when they are annoyed is debatable. It may be unique to Trinidad. The teachers, from elementary to high school had labelled "steupsing" as "sucking your teeth." It was met with severe punishment. Sister Marguerite didn't hear the steupses either. She went on and on.

"If you don't learn to sew and do fine embroidery, you will not be able to find good husbands. Men do not want girls who are not good in the housewifely arts."

At this, Angela commented to Tessa, "And you can do such fine embroidery, and look where you ended up."

Tessa giggled, but was afraid to say anything. The thought of Sister Marguerite as a young girl looking for a husband was too much.

Nora began to cry. A Black girl from Tessa's neighbourhood, Nora came from a crowded compound with many families in it. She was trying hard to cry quietly, but bit by bit her sobs became louder. She had remembered to ask her mother for the needlework fee, but the money was just not available.

Sister Marguerite called Nora to the teacher's desk. Nora made her way haltingly and shakily to the front of the room. Tessa was thinking that poor Nora was already crying—what more could the nun say or do to her? The teachers' desks were placed on a podium so there was always a clear view of the entire classroom. It gave a dignity to the teacher and created a fearful distance between teacher and students.

Sister Marguerite put her arm around Nora and said, "I don't mean you. Don't cry. It's those others who are too lazy and careless to remember that I am mad at."

She looked pointedly at Gloria de la Rosa, whose parents were known to be extremely wealthy. They owned large coconut estates and had interests in almost every successful enterprise on the island.

Tessa realized that Sister Marguerite knew that Nora's tears meant that she had not been able to afford the needlework fee. Since everyone wore the same school uniform, there was no way of discerning the wealth of one's family. And all the Black girls were not necessarily poor. Sister Marguerite gave Nora the tea towel she was to embroider, telling her that she should bring the money next week, and sent her back to her seat. Tessa was impressed that Sister Marguerite was astute enough to realize the real reason for Nora's tears.

Nora was to run into another problem soon after this, this time not with a nun but with one of the lay teachers. Every Monday morning, the students handed in their long compositions that they worked on every weekend. They began these in class on Friday. One day Nora did not have a copy book in which to do her composition, so Tessa gave her one.

Nora handed in her composition on Monday, neglecting to cross out Tessa's name on the front of the book and replace it with her own. When she was handing back their corrected compositions on Wednesday, Miss Green, a woman from England who taught them English, called Tessa to the front of the room. On questioning Tessa as to why there were two copybooks with her name on them, and being told that one belonged to Nora, she summoned Nora to her desk. Everyone knew the girls were in trouble. Somebody must have copied someone else's composition. Some *"uh-huh's"* were quietly murmured by those who couldn't keep their feelings to themselves. The whole class was paying attention, Tessa knew. She was embarrassed at being singled out like this.

Miss Green was short, stocky, and plain with a large bosom. There was nothing pretty or soft about her, neither her hair nor her eyes. Her clothes, too, were severe and usually dark in colour. In a country where the children were used to seeing their teachers, as long as they were not nuns, wearing bright, fashionable clothes, they found her outfits unfashionably plain and boring. She intimidated the students with her fine English accent and her use of the language.

The rest of the class pretended to be writing, but instead were listening intently. They were only in the first term of their first year. Cheating so soon? "I lent her one of my copybooks," Tessa explained. "She did not have enough."

"And why did she not have enough copybooks? You were given a list with the number of books required. Why didn't you bring all the books you were told?"

Nora hung her head. Tessa remembered that on their first day of school, while they were taking a pirate taxi to school together, Nora had told Tessa that her mother had not bought twelve copybooks for her, as she thought twelve was an extravagant number. Nora did not say this to Miss Green.

They tried to explain again. Nora, a heavy and slow-speaking girl, was no real help.

Tessa said, "I only lent her my copybook. She was going to give me back a new one when she got one. But she didn't cross off my name on the front and put her own."

It was no use. The woman had already decided what she would do.

"I really don't understand what the problem is," Miss Green told them. "I still don't know whose composition is whose. How am I supposed to know? For this stupidity, both of you girls will be given a zero for this week's composition." Tessa knew that if a student got too many zeros then she would be called out in front of the whole school and walk the terrifying distance from the back of the long hall and stand in front of the seated phalanx of nuns and lay teachers. Then she must bow in shame and disgrace to the Reverend Mother. This was a woman who was seen only once a month at these assemblies. You would then be spoken to in a tone of great sorrow and gentleness, which made you vow to yourself it would never happen again; just seeing the sadness in her eyes was enough. Sumintra Maharaj, who had been "called out" in the first term, had told Tessa how bad the experience was. Sumintra said that she had lost so many marks for punctuality. This was because she lived far away in the country and, after coming on the train, she had to walk several few miles from the station to the convent, and so was often late. Tessa wondered how she ever made it on time at all, and why her parents couldn't give her money for a taxi fare. The pirate taxis plied on most routes and were as cheap as the buses. But Tessa realized that Sumintra must be a scholarship student, a College Exhibitioner, and very poor, and she shouldn't ask her about taking taxis.

Tessa knew that if she was "called out," there was a danger that the teachers and nuns would classify her as an idler and a bad student, which could affect her results and ultimately her ambition to succeed in life She would not be able to do something great, as she had always dreamed. Even if she couldn't become a writer like Jo in *Little Women*, at least she could have a career of some kind, an opportunity her mother and aunts never had. To have a life where every penny did not have to be watched. A life filled with good music, books, and a beautiful house with fine furniture and dishes. A world where people spoke to each other in soft and civilized tones. In good English, not in dialect. Where people did not shout and bawl you out, causing you to feel bad for making a simple mistake. Where people did not bully. This was a life she had only had glimpses of, one she knew that others enjoyed even on their little island. This was the kind of life that was depicted in the movies she went to on the weekends, when her mother could spare the money. To belong to a world where such lives would be the prerogative not only of the white and wealthy, but of people like her. This was her dream. She would make this her goal in life, she vowed to herself.

Would people like Miss Green thwart her ambitions? How difficult would it be to succeed in life if one kept on meeting Miss Greens and her ilk? And did it mean that in order to succeed one must not help others since it could get you in trouble? Though she resented Nora's carelessness in not writing her name on the cover of the book, Tessa knew that Miss Green had been grossly unfair to both of them. All her life, Tessa had been taught to practice the virtue of charity. Her mother had shown her children by example by not only giving her "widow's mite" to those less fortunate, but by always showing kindness and helpfulness to others.

When their neighbour, Mr. Harris, passed away, his relative Alice, who had lived with him for many years, was evicted, and her belongings thrown into the street. Mr Harris had lived and worked in the United States for many years and Mr Harris, according to the neighbours, had willed his house to his church, an American evangelical church. On seeing Alice in such a plight, Lucille, her children, and some of the other neighbours went to help her retrieve her possessions. Tom, the next-door neighbour, offered his truck to move Alice to her daughter's house. For the rest of her life, Tessa would never forget the picture of Alice, sitting on the sidewalk, surrounded by everything she owned and sobbing uncontrollably. From that day on, Tessa was mortally afraid that something like that might happen to her in the future. How does one protect oneself against destitution like that? she wondered. Clyde and Lucille and the two girls were appalled at the lack of charity the church had shown in their treatment of Alice, throwing her out on to the street like a beggar.

Tessa knew that the essence of their own religion was the virtue of charity. She had learned at church *"that if a man had many virtues but not that of charity he was no more than sounding brass or a tinkling cymbal."* And this virtue of charity was what her family practised by coming to Alice's aid. And the other neighbours—all of different religions, or none at all—had risen to the challenge of helping a woman in need. Thinking about Alice's story, Tessa wondered if the situation with Nora was any different. Should she, like the travellers in the story of The Good Samaritan, have looked straight ahead and ignored the bloodied man by the wayside? Was this the way to success? By not being a good samaritan? Tessa was too humiliated to tell anyone at home what had happened. They all expected her to succeed, and she did not want to burden them with this. And there was no one in the class who suggested that she should complain to the principal that an injustice had been done. It was the 1950s. Students never imagined they could have rights. And non-white girls in a school that had once been excluisvely for "whites only" even less so.

11.
The Status Quo

SINGING WAS AN integral part of the curriculum. The school choir earned first place in the music festival every year, but it was made up of mostly white and light-skinned girls. The few Black or East Indian girls would be ones with extraordinarily good singing voices. When she began to attend the convent, it dawned on Tessa that her cousin, Camille, was in the choir not only because of her good singing voice, but because her complexion was fair. Though Camille's cousin, Priscilla, had a good voice too, her complexion was dark.

Tessa's class was at their obligatory weekly singing lesson. Sister Joseph was stern and never let the girls get away with any "slack" behaviour. She pushed them to the limit, and no one dared to cross her. For such a tiny person, she exerted an extraordinary strength. The girls feared her sharp tongue but learned to respect her skills in teaching them how to sing. One day, however, Sister Joseph, referring to a student who wasn't singing in tune said, "I don't think Chinese people can sing very well, as they have such small mouths."

There was silence in the room. All the pupils of the Sacred Heart Convent were proud to be there and knew they were privileged. At home, they were constantly cautioned about the dangers of "talking back" to their teachers and especially to the nuns. It was drummed into them that success lay in not rocking the boat, not complaining or ever criticizing the powers that be. Many of their fathers and brothers came home from work seething at insults and unfair treatment in their civil service and teaching jobs, but their children learned that there was no use in fighting back. That this was the fate of the Black and East Indian in a country still ruled by England. A country in which society was highly stratified, not only on the basis of wealth but also on the basis of skin colouur and the straightness of one's hair. In order to get ahead, one had to swallow one's pride. Questioning or contradicting one's teachers in a colonial territory amounted to social suicide. After the music lesson, as they walked back to their classroom, Tessa and her friends, all Black and mixed-race girls, could not stop obsessing about the remark. Race was a sensitive issue, and though it permeated every facet of the lives of the people on the island, it was usually talked about only in the privacy of drawing rooms, and only among close friends and family.

Annabel James, an outspoken Black girl, whom everyone, students and teachers alike, labelled as "don't carish" because she was often in trouble for refusing to submit to rules she found stupid or useless, said to the girls walking next to her, "We should go and see Reverend Mother and tell her that Sister Joseph has gone too far this time."

Brenda and Tessa, who were always afraid to cause trouble, remained quiet. But Gloria Simmons, a brown-skinned girl whose father was in the higher echelons of the civil service and who was usually more interested in having fun than in defying authority, said, cynically, "And you think that will change Sister Joseph's attitude? Reverend Mother, though she's a nice lady, won't do anything. Don't forget, she's white too. And anyway, how we going to ask for permission to go and see her? What reason we will give? We can't just walk into the nun's quarters; we're not allowed there. Forget it, let the Chinese girls go see her if they want. But Chinese people don't worry about things like that. How you think they get rich? By keeping their mouths shut and selling to everybody in their lil' shops and parlours in every corner of the island and now they own a lot of import-export business and all kinds of big companies."

Brenda said, in her quiet, diffident way, "What about going to see the principal, Sister Aloysius?"

Tessa snorted, "I would never go and see *her*. She doesn't care about people like us. You ever see which girls always hanging around her? Is only white and half-white girls who are her pets. Her father is a big important man on the island. You know what her name was before she became a nun? It was Fitzmaurice. You know how rich they are? But why she call herself Aloysius? Why not Catherine or Margaret or Anne after some female saint instead of a male?"

Tessa was to rue this remark as the school year came to an end.

By the time they reached their classroom, Annabel had "cooled down." She was always lighting fires about racism, about fairness and justice, and about the nuns' treatment of the minority of Black girls. She was known as a rebel. Her uniform sometimes looked as though it had been slept in, her *watcheconges* were always scruffy, and her hair was often untidy. She didn't care for all the stuffy rules they were required to follow about punctuality, clean uniforms, and length of skirt, or about the ban against wearing nail polish or jewellery. Several times her name had been called out at the assembly for an accumulation of these offences. Though she had been threatened with expulsion, nothing had been done about it. It was because she was so smart they knew she might win the only girls' scholarship to an English University and thus bring glory to the school.

Tessa could only imagine how the Chinese girls felt about Sister Joseph's comment, but none of them were her friends because of the existing racial hierarchy: English, French-Creole, Portuguese, Syrian, Chinese, Venezuelan. The Venezuelans were boarders and rumbled around the halls of the convent rattling away in their Venezuelan Spanish. Lower down the ladder were darker-skinned mulatto girls whose parents were comfortable but not rich, and, at the very bottom, came the Blacks and East Indians who had no money or social position.

Tessa and her friends had concluded that the nuns who were "local whites" often showed more prejudice towards the non-white girls than the Irish nuns, and that Sister Joseph, the music teacher, was the most extreme example. But this theory did not always hold water. One of the Irish nuns, Sister Philomena, the domestic science teacher, was loud and abusive to anyone who made a mistake. The white girls had enough self-esteem not to let it bother them, but Tessa would become nervous in the kitchen and drop things or forget some of the rules because she was scared of her. Sister Philomena would say things like, "These are scones, and they are properly aerated, not like these bakes people make in this country." Tessa thought this was a strange thing to say since she had seen her mother and aunts made different kinds of bakes—*roti*, johnny bakes, and fried bakes—and they all contained baking powder.

In their cooking classes, they learned to make *blancmange*, beef steak, English puddings, cakes, and pies, but no Caribbean food. Tessa never saw her mother use a cookbook. She never saw adults exchanging written recipes; all the recipes they used were from memory or shared orally. At home, mothers did not measure ingredients but instead used handfuls of flour or rice and "averaged" things like baking powder, lard, or butter. As for the beloved *roti*, which later became famous in many parts of the world, none of the written recipes seemed to work. It was a magic formula, the secret held only by a few Moslem men who made over-sized *rotis* for weddings, tender soft flatbreads as light as air and flakier than puff pastry. Or by women who ply their trade at roadside stalls. Or by grandmothers whose skill will die with them, since their grandchildren were too busy becoming doctors and lawyers and teachers and CEOs to acquire the humble *roti*-making skill.

One day Brenda became the object of Sister Philomena's wrath. Brenda had made scrambled eggs. The class period would soon come to an end, so the serving and the clean-up had to be finished within a few minutes.

Brenda had grabbed the first plate she could find in which to serve her scrambled eggs.

"You are using a soup plate! To serve scrambled eggs!" the nun screamed.

Brenda saw all the plates in the kitchen as good plates. She didn't know the difference between a soup plate and a dinner plate. Neither did Tessa, for that matter. Tessa began to understand that the rest of the world did not live like the poor people in Trinidad. Most people had a few good plates they used for visitors. Plates that were not enamel, but were not fine china either. The words "fine china" were not part of their vocabulary. And they knew that in the countryside, people did not even have enamel plates, but still used bowls, plates, and cups fashioned from the fruit of the *calabash* tree, a utensil used by the Aboriginal Indians, which made perfect eating dishes. *Calabashes* were large round gourds that, with the seeds and pulp scooped out, could be cut into bowls, plates, and cups.

Though Tessa knew it was an honour to attend the Sacred Heart Convent and she was proud to be seen in the bright blue belted tunic and white blouse with its neat Peter Pan collar, she had a gnawing suspicion that something was missing in the education she was receiving. One day, as she and Sylvia were doing their homework on the table in the drawing room, and Clyde was sitting nearby reading the *Evening News*, she said to him, "Why I have to study three foreign languages and no history?"

"That's because the nuns and priests don't want you to know about the scandals and corruption in the Catholic Church in the Middle Ages," he replied.

"The Presbyterian schools have debating, but not us," continued Tessa. "And why only the boys at the college across the way put on Shakespeare plays every year? We only do

Gilbert and Sullivan, and that is only for the choir. And the choir is only for the white girls, and those who can sing like opera stars."

Tessa felt cheated. Though she did not have an extraordinary voice, she had a good ear and learned tunes very quickly. She knew all the words of the popular songs she heard on the radio, and at home she sang all the time. She had always sung in the class choirs at the school in San Juan de la Pina. One year the school choir performed in a community concert held at the school. Her mother had to sew a new white dress for her to wear for the concert, which was a big event in the district. For the children taking part, however, it turned out to be a long and tiring evening. The organizers, in their wisdom, had put the nine-year-old girls in the second to last place on the program. The children had waited outside in the heat of the tropical afternoon—dressed in their hot and frilly taffeta dresses with puffy sleeves that itched their arms, and satin sashes that stuck to their waists in the heat—while the adults sang solos and duets, whole choirs of men and women performed, and old men dressed in their best black suits played piano, violin, or flute solos.

Besides singing in the class choirs at the San Juan de la Pina School, Tessa was always chosen to do the class recitation at school concerts. For these she had learned long and involved poems which, from the age of eight, she had recited in front of the entire school. Whenever the Inspector came, she was the one chosen to read for him. She loved performing and reading out loud. Why didn't she have the chance to memorize lines and act in a play? Instead of singing or acting, she had to learn all these tedious declensions and conjugations. And why was it that only the Venezuelan boarders and some of the white girls played tennis after school, while the only sport the non-white girls played was netball? She had tried to play once and soon gave it up. She found netball boring because she had to stand in the centre and run for the ball. She was not aggressive enough to get the ball. And why did some girls leave during class time for music lessons from one of the nuns?

Clyde was getting up to go. He didn't really need to sit at that table to do his homework since there was a study hall at his school, but he often would help his sisters if they needed it.

"I know what you mean," he added. "I wish I was a Presbyterian like my friend Henry. The Presbyterians have youth groups, and they play sports at the back of their church in Meadowbrook. Our church have nothing like that. They used to have a Catholic Youth Organization, but the Archbishop banned it because all the girls got pregnant."

"What?" Tessa and Sylvia giggled at the thought.

"I bet that only happen in the country churches," Sylvia said, "because they have a lot of empty space and bushes and mangrove to go and hide in to do their business. Where we will go? Everybody bound to see."

Clyde and Tessa both laughed at this. "You real funny, yes, Sylvia," he said. "You always coming up with this kind of thing."

So is that *why* their church never offered any social activities for them? Tessa thought. And so now they had to find their own.

Clyde left soon after.

"Why boys can go up the Main Road and we have to sit here every night?" Tessa asked her mother who had just come into the drawing room.

"You want to go *liming* up the Main Road with the boys? You know any decent girls who out of the house after six o'clock at night when it already dark? You just asking for trouble if you do that. Only loose women, not young girls out on the Main Road after six." Six o'clock was the cut-off time for coming home, since in tropical Trinidad the sun always went down at that time.

Lucille Joseph looked stern, as she always did whenever she set down rules like these. Tessa and Sylvia nudged each other, a gesture they used whenever they thought their mother's ideas outdated, and they had to gang up against her.

"But it's so boring here, night after night. And weekends too," Tessa whined.

In her first term, Tessa had wanted to join the Girl Guides. She was tactfully steered away from it by the nun in charge, who had suggested that the uniform would be an additional expense for her family. Tessa half agreed with her. The convent required four uniforms: the everyday blue tunic with its white blouse; the white one-piece cotton cookery uniform; a dress uniform consisting of a grey-belted white linen tunic and a white shirt; and a grey cotton tunic with a blue belt and a white shirt for physical education. The dress uniform would only be used a few times in the year. But the most useless one, Tessa thought, was the phys. ed. uniform. The teacher had taught ballet so she had them do a few ballet exercises at their weekly class, which was held in the same hall where the singing lessons took place. That the girls be taught to play field hockey or netball outside in the fresh air of the eternal summer was unthinkable, since they become hot and sweaty and the school had no shower facilities. So the ballet exercises were the extent of their physical education.

But Tessa had been a Girl Guide at the San Juan de la Pina School. And dearly wished to continue. Their Guide mistress, Miss Gardiner, a Black woman from a wealthy family, rode a Harley-Davidson, which had been imported especially for her. She was the first woman in the island to ride a motorcycle. She was a warm and caring woman who lived in St. Elizabeth Park, a prosperous part of town, and she came to this lower-class neighbourhood to run a Girl Guide company. There were only six girls in the troupe: Tessa, Brenda, and four other girls. But Tessa loved going every Monday after school. At home, there was only the radio for entertainment and a constant array of mundane household tasks. Miss Gardiner took them to her father's cocoa estate for a weekend of camping where they cooked, in layers of brown paper on an open campfire, the best beef Tessa ever tasted. There were jamborees at the guide hut, Saturday outings, and the challenge of working for various badges. Now there would be no more campfire singing and no more weekend camping trips, all the joys of guiding that she had come to love. And without Girl Guides she had no other school activities like those the white girls enjoyed—no singing, no tennis, no plays. Tessa felt that there was a hole in her social life, and, like Clyde, she often wished she was Presbyterian and not Roman Catholic.

12.
Empire Day

THE EMPIRE DAY PARADE was a key event in the school year for all the schools in the town of Port of Spain. The children all went to the grounds of the Queen's Royal College, a prestigious boys' school, to march in the parade. Then they stood at attention for the Governor to give the salute while the police band played "Land of Hope and Glory" and "God Save the Queen."

Tessa and Brenda, dressed in their school uniforms, took a pirate taxi and went to march in the parade. The children had to wait for a long time in the midday sun for it to get underway. The Guide and Scout troops from all the schools were there. Tessa spotted Clyde and thought he looked very handsome in his Sea Scout uniform.

"There's my brother," she said excitedly to the girls standing nearby. Policemen on horseback were keeping order, and there was loud chattering until the parade started.

Many vendors lined up their carts and trucks outside the college grounds and waited for the parade to end so they could sell their wares. The men sold ice cream and popsicles, which the islanders called "pallets." The women were selling local sweets including tamarind balls, guava cheese, and pawpaw balls. Orange sellers with huge juicy navel oranges were waiting with sharp knives to peel and slice the oranges for customers. The female vendors sat on rickety wooden folding chairs, their heads were covered with African-style turbans. The coconut vendors, all male, stood by their donkey carts, which were piled high with fresh green coconuts. With one adroit swing of their sharp cutlasses, the vendors would slice off the heads of the coconuts and, in another swift motion, the now decapitated coconut, would be turned over and the sweet water poured into a glass for the customer to drink. They hardly spilled any of that precious water. Then, laying the coconut on the ground, they would chop its heavy impenetrable shell into two and carve out a small makeshift spoon from the coconut shell. The white, delicious, soft jelly inside could be eaten with the handmade spoon. Since the children were not allowed to eat and drink during the parade, no matter how hungry and thirsty they got, they watched the treats with longing eyes, waiting for the long, hot, and tiring event to end.

Tessa and Brenda weren't sure if they had enough money to buy coconuts, and they were too timid to ask because there were so many big boys crowding around the coconut vendors' carts. They thought the boys might push them around. Or maybe the vendors would overcharge them, seeing they were two young girls. So they contented themselves with a Coca-Cola, cold and dripping, from the vendor's cooler and went to another stall to buy a sugarcake, which was made of coconut and sugar and then boiled for a long time into a solid consistency, flavoured with vanilla essence, and coloured with red, white, or green food colouring. Sugarcakes were cheap.

Tessa would have liked a currant roll, made of light flaky pastry, but when they stopped at that stall, the woman selling the currant rolls said to them, "Hurry up. What all yuh want? Make up your mind quick."

Tessa was offended and though that even if she had the money she wouldn't buy anything from this woman. So when the woman said, "Is a shilling for one," Tessa looked at Brenda and they both walked away. "Let her keep her stinking currant roll," Brenda said indignantly.

"The currants will rot and fall off before anybody buy from *she*," Tessa added, giggling at the thought of the currants, like little flies all over the pastry, fermenting and dying. The "she" seemed more appropriate than "her," as dialect was the only thing to use when one got properly angry.

When Tessa returned home, Lucille was in the kitchen making guava jam. Sylvia was sitting at the table with a classic comic book, *The Count of Monte Cristo*. Ever since they had discovered these classic comics, Tessa and Sylvia had gorged themselves on them. They read *The Last of the Mohicans, The Corsican Brothers, The Three Musketeers, Les Misérables*, and other famous novels in comic form. Some parents did not allow their children to read any comics, for teachers didn't approve of them, but Lucille was not one of those over-zealous parents. She also allowed her children go to the cinema and to play card games. Card games were considered evil by some parents, but not by Lucille. She was anything but a Puritan. She enjoyed a good joke as well as the wit and risqué humour of calypsoes.

"All the students and the Scout and Guide troops from every school in Port of Spain were there except for Meadowbrook School," Tessa announced as she got herself a glass of water and some sweet biscuits to eat.

"I think it's because all the nuns in my school are Irish," said Sylvia. "Many of the nuns at your school come from the local English people. The Irish don't care too much for the Queen."

"And you know what, Mum? Remember Sister Barnabas discouraged me from joining the Guides because she said the uniform would be one more expense for my family? Well, today I found out why she didn't want me. It's because everybody in the convent Guide troupe is white. Except for one Black girl. I don't know why Teresa Campbell is there."

"I know why," put in Sylvia. "You see, her aunt, Sister Lawrence, is a nun, not in the order of the Sacred Heart—the nuns who run your school, they only accept whites—but in the Holy Ghost order. They take everybody, of all colours. And so they had to let her into the Guide troupe because of her aunt. You know, all those church people stick together."

"Well, that's how it is in this country and in your school, my child. I'm afraid it's what we have to put up with, people like us," said Lucille.

"You won't believe how many children fainted and had to go in the St. John's Ambulance van," continued Tessa. "All of us were sweating like pigs, the sun was so hot. And I was tired. Me and Brenda had to walk from the Main Road, where the taxi dropped us, all the way to the college grounds, because the taxi didn't go there."

"Why they make the children march in that hot sun every year?" Lucille grumbled. Her children had been obliged to do that even in elementary school. "Why our children must go through all this trouble for a queen far away in England? It's real stupidness, you hear?" she muttered angrily.

Tessa had heard her mother's annual rant about the Empire Day parade often enough over the years. But this year she said to Lucille, "Mum, but you who like the royal family so much, complaining about the parade? You always reading the newspaper and then telling us about all the things the royal family doing and which castle they spending time at. You know the names of all of the royal family, all Queen Mary's children, and even which members of the royal families all over Europe are related to each other. And you always quoting the Duke of Windsor when he said he could not continue to be king, 'without the help and support of the woman I love.'"

Her remarks about the Empire Day parade were just another contradiction in her mother's character, Tessa thought. And the one Black girl in the convent Girl Guide troupe was there only because her aunt was a nun? The world was such a confusing place. Adults were always saying one thing and doing another. She couldn't wait to be an adult so that she could decide things for herself and not have to follow the rules of grown-ups, which changed with their every whim, or which did not always make sense.

13.
Of Carnival Queens, Americans and Impossible Dreams

T HE JUNIOR CHAMBER OF COMMERCE Carnival Queen Contest, known as the Jaycees Contest, was fast approaching. In the library one day, when no class was there and the room was quiet, Tessa was shocked to overhear a conversation between Sister Philomena and Margaret La Roche. Margaret had graduated the year before from the convent. Tessa wondered what kind of girl would come back and visit Sister Philomena, of all the nuns in the school. Most of the girls hated her. Margaret was a contestant this year in the Jaycees Carnival Queen pageant.

"So, tell me about your costume," Tessa heard Sister Philomena ask Margaret.

"I'm supposed to be Cleopatra," said Margaret. "My costume is a champagne colour. The top is a sleeveless, low-cut, V-neck blouse. It's fitted below the bust and trimmed with three-inch gold braid. I wear a wide, jewelled, Egyptian-style collar. My midriff is exposed, and the waist of the pants is also trimmed with gold braid, and encrusted with jewels. I wear shorts underneath since the skirt is really only a long sheer piece of soft, transparent material—I think it's georgette—and opens out at the sides. It's copied from a famous painting by Jean-Léon Gérôme called *Cleopatra Before Caesar*. The golden headband, too, is decorated with many coloured stones. I also wear a wide, snake bracelet on my arm, a gold ankle band, and Eastern-style sandals. Lucky my hair is long, so I am going to comb it into a low bun at the nape of my neck. And since I'm Cleopatra, it's good I have black and not blonde hair. I went for the fitting of my costume yesterday and I just love it."

"It sounds lovely," said Sister Philomena. "And what about your evening dress? What style is it?"

"It's pale blue. The strapless bodice is lace and the skirt is satin, and it has a crinoline underneath so it spreads out all around. I have to learn to walk in it with the high heels, and this woman, Adele de la Cruz, who was once a model in New York, is teaching us how to walk properly as we cross the stage. Now she has her own modelling agency in Port of Spain. Oh, wait, I think I have the sketches of the costume and evening gown here. They were designed by my Aunt Louisa. She's an artist and she had an exhibition in London last year." Margaret rummaged in her purse and pulled out the sketches.

The Jaycees Queen contest was denounced from the Catholic Church pulpits every year. The priests contended that the girls were being paraded like cattle in the marketplace and it was beneath their human dignity. The nuns, too, opposed it stridently. But year after year, ex-students from the two convent schools and the Anglican Girls' School were the main contestants as the prizes were exorbitant: trips to New York or London, cars, clothes, luggage, cosmetics. But, one of the unwritten rules of the contest was that beauty belonged only to those girls who were white or nearly white.

Tessa, consumed with curiosity, moved towards where Sister Philomena and Margaret were sitting and pretended to be looking for a book in the shelves behind them. She hope to peek at the sketches and be able to boast that she had seen the outfits of a Carnival Queen contestant before the big night. Sister Philomena and Margaret had their backs to the shelves. One was so intent on showing the sketches, the other on perusing them, that Tessa was able to catch a glimpse of the outfits without either of them realizing what she was up to. Tessa thought the Cleopatra costume looked more like something a harem girl would wear, or even someone like Salome, but no one would dare wear a Salome costume. That would be going too far.

"I'm sure you'll win the title," Sister Philomena said encouragingly. "Didn't your sister win last year?"

"No, that was my cousin. My sister won two years ago. I hope I can follow in her footsteps."

Tessa thought it was strange that a girl running in the Jaycees Contest was welcomed back as a visitor to the convent. Instead here was this nun talking to her former student with admiration in her voice, almost as if she too wanted to be at the Queen's Park Savannah cheering Margaret as she crossed the stage. Tessa's could picture Sister Philomena sitting in the stands at the Queen's Park Savannah. The long white habit would be most incongruous in the den of iniquity that was the Carnival Queen contest, she mused. At this thought, Tessa smothered the laugh that threatened to overwhelm her.

It was too late. Both Sister Philomena and Margaret looked up and saw her. Tessa had been so absorbed in listening to them and looking at the sketches that she had forgotten her pretence of looking for a book. Her cover was broken.

"What are you doing there?" the nun said sharply. "Why aren't you in class?

"Miss de Vere sent me to find a book from the library," Tessa quickly replied.

"Well, where is the book? I don't see you looking for any book. You just standing there, minding other people's business. You're such a stupid girl. Can't do the right thing in the kitchen, and can't even find a book. Hurry up and get back to your class. I'll report you to the principal if you don't take care."

So, Tessa thought, as she left the library like a dog with her tail between her legs, were the exhortations not to take part in beauty contests only for the non-white girls? And why would Sister Philomena show so much interest in Margaret's outfits if the church considered the contest sinful? Perhaps Sister Philomena didn't know how the church felt about the contest.

But Tessa shrugged that thought off. She must know. Didn't she have to follow all the rules the Archbishop laid down? And didn't those rules come from far away Rome? From the Vatican? As for non-white girls entering the contest, it was out of the question, for they knew they would never win, even if they could find a sponsor.

One year, however, an East Indian girl, sponsored by some newly rich Indian businessman from the oil-rich south of the island, was a Queen contestant. She arrived late, and, listening to the descriptions of the dresses and costumes on the radio, Tessa realized that the girl must have put on a poor show. Her sponsors from the south must not have been aware of the intricacies of the contest. And not making sure that she was on time? In later years, a few East Indian girls became Jaycee Queens, but they usually had almost white or light brown complexions so their looks approached European standards.

By the time Tessa had gotten much older, the Indians began to have their own beauty contests—Miss Trinidad India they called it. It might as well have been the Jaycees Contest all over again, though, as the contestants were usually girls with fair complexions, never those with brown or dark skins.

The Sunday night of the Carnival weekend, Tessa, Sylvia, and her mother were at their Aunt Marjorie's. They had gone to listen to the broadcast of the Carnival Queen contest on Radio Trinidad. Aunt Marjorie's children, Laurel and Cynthia, were there too; the families were making an evening of it. Aunt Marjorie's husband had died the year before, and the lower level of their huge, beautiful, two-storey house overlooking the sea had been converted into a dry goods store and a food store called a parlour. The parlour sold soft drinks, ice, bread, cigarettes, sweets, and inexpensive, heavy sweet buns known as *bellyfulls*. It was eight o'clock. The store and parlour were closed for the day, and the adults and children were huddled around the radio in the back room of the store waiting for the contest to begin.

Suddenly, there was a knock on the large glass front door. Everyone looked at each other. Should they take the chance of going to the door? They were all women. What if it was a burglar with a gun? Or a drunk? Aunt Marjorie approached the door cautiously. She turned on the outside light, and peered out. There stood a tall American soldier in an officer's uniform. With him was a beautiful woman in an elaborate sea-green strapless evening gown of satin with a wide, crinoline skirt. Aunt Marjorie opened the door and let them in. These two would pose no threat, and they had stopped at her store because they needed something.

The children stared in awe. They had never seen people dressed like this in real life, only in the cinema.

"Would you be able to help us?" the officer asked. "We saw the light, even though your shop is closed. My wife has a problem with her dress. Would you be so kind as to fix it for her?"

The woman turned around and showed Aunt Marjorie the bustle at the back of her skirt. The stitching had come loose, and she was in dire need of a needle and thread.

They had come to the right place. There would be no more stores like this before they got to the American naval base, where they were headed, only the long stretch of road bordering the sea. The Americans were lucky; Aunt Marjorie was an accomplished seamstress.

Aunt Marjorie did not even ask the woman to remove her dress. She was able, without poking her with the needle, to quickly sew up the offending bustle.

The officer and his wife thanked her profusely. He put his hand in his pocket, drew out his wallet, and proffered a note. It looked like twenty American dollars, not a small sum. Aunt Marjorie shook her head.

"No, no, it's all right. It was not a big problem," she said to them. "I don't need any payment."

This was part of the code of conduct of all the aunts, Tessa thought. They were always too proud to accept anything that smacked of charity. Tessa knew that things were not easy for Aunt Marjorie financially since her husband's death. She wondered why her aunt would refuse the money. The man did not insist, and they drove away. Tessa was sure that the next week her cousins would tell her that the Americans had come by again with a gift or with more money. But no such visit occurred. "They did not even stop by to say hello," said Laurel, as she and Tessa talked about the incident the next week. Everyone knew how rich the American soldiers were. They shimmied around the island in their jeeps, trucks, and cars; they built roads; they cleared land with huge bulldozers; and they threw their money around carelessly, especially on local women of the night. They always had cigarettes to hand out to the locals and chewing gum for the children. The Americans, in leasing the land for their naval base, brought their prosperity and their arrogance to Trinidadians who, in turn, began to thumb their noses at the people of the "small islands," who were not so lucky.

They should have come back, Tessa thought, and brought some small token of appreciation to her aunt.

As the announcers excitedly described the Carnival Queen costumes, Tessa waited impatiently for Margaret la Roche to walk across the stage. When she finally did so, there were many oohs and aahs from the announcers and the audience. The announcer, Janet Marryat, explained that this costume had been copied from a painting called Cleopatra Before Caesar, naming the famous artist who had painted this picture of Cleopatra as she was being unrolled from a carpet and presented to Caesar. Mrs. Marryat, however, declared that in her opinion, the costume was good enough, even though it was authentic. "Remember," she commented, "the judges like to see lots of leg, and this costume covers up too much of this contestant's legs. The colours are beautiful, and so is the contestant, but I can't see her walking away with the crown."

Indeed, it was Annette De Silva, whose costume was a one-piece bathing suit with a wide, colourful headpiece portraying a scarlet ibis, the most beautiful of local birds, who won the title that year. Her gold satin evening gown was a strapless and had a wide crinolined skirt, and she had looked regal.

Tessa later learned through Angela—who had some friends among the white girls, and from whom Tessa always heard the latest gossip concerning those in high society—that Margaret's Aunt Louisa had said that Trinidadian people were too uncultured to appreciate the artistry of her design. Did they know of famous art works found in the Museums of London and Paris, like she did? And who were the judges anyway? "Nouveau-riche" businessmen who had made lots of money but had no appreciation of culture. "None of them were from the old aristocracy of the island, people like us," she said, "descended from French Royalists with centuries of breeding behind us."

The next day, Sylvia came home from school crying bitterly. This was a complete shock to Tessa as she firmly believed in the safety and respectability of their neighbourhood.

Tessa, Clyde, and their mother formed a protective circle around her, as if, by doing so, they could alleviate some of the pain she was suffering. Tessa was scared. Sylvia seldom cried. She was always the strong and unflappable one.

"What happened to you?" their mother asked her. "What you crying for?"

"Petra Hernandez say that I steal her bicycle," Sylvia sobbed, "and the nuns keep my bike. I had to walk home."

The white blouse of her school uniform was soaked in sweat. It was a long walk from the school back to their home, and no one, if they could help it, ever walked that distance in the tropical afternoon sun.

"What? Petra must be mad to say a thing like that," her mother said indignantly. "Every morning you ride to school, and she living in the next street. You mean to tell me she never see you riding your own bicycle every day as you go down the Silk Cotton Road? Why she would accuse you of stealing hers? And the nuns believe her because she white like them? I have a good mind to go to the school right now and tell those nuns what I think of them. "

But she never did. It was Clyde who went and told the nuns that his sister owned her own bike. Since he was attending the neighbouring Catholic College of Our Lady of Lourdes, they accepted his word. Why this accusation had been made in the first place, the Josephs were never to know. The Hernandez family lived on the prosperous adjoining street of Silk Cotton Road and were neighbours to Aunt Marjorie. The Hernandezes had often seen the Joseph children visiting their cousins. And the three families attended the same neighbourhood Catholic church.

Every time something like this happened, Tessa's stomach felt like it was turning over and everything in it threatening to come out. Why was her family always being victimized by people of other races? Why did everyone feel they had power over them? Was there any place in the world where people were treated fairly and with dignity? she wondered. Or was everywhere in the world the same, with people hurting each other and spreading lies for no reason? And being part of the same church didn't seem to make any difference when it came to racism and bullying.

14.

Cockroach in the Fowl Party

I N HER SECOND YEAR at Convent of the Sacred Heart, Tessa and Angela Spence became close friends. Angela was from Meadowbrook. She had white skin, but her hair was "pressed" or straightened with a hot comb. Tessa and Angela were often at the back of the room having fun, paying little attention to the teacher at the front, but they were always careful not to be found out. Tessa would often stop off in the pirate taxi, which plied the Main Road between San Juan de la Pina and Meadowbrook, to visit Angela's house after school. She would then return home before it was dark.

Tessa had made the mistake of asking Angela about the Venezuelan boy she had seen in the group of boys and girls with Angela. Tessa thought he was cute. His name was Roberto Cadiz. They were all at a bingo being held at Our Lady of Lourdes College. Bingo was something new to the island and this was a big social event. Everyone was dressed in their finest. Once Angela realized that Tessa had her eye on Roberto, she kept whispering "Roberto, Roberto" in Tessa's ear whenever she could. Tessa got tired of it and wished she hadn't said anything to Angela.

Even when they were in the chapel, where they prayed the Litany of the Saints and they had to respond, "Have mercy on us," Angela would tease her with the words, "Have mercy on Roberto." Tessa was embarassed and feared that one of the nuns would hear. The chapel was a place where it was impossible to suppress giggles or laughter whenever it came upon you. It was as though the quiet and solemnity created a tension that could only be relieved by giggling or laughing. One day Angela had a laughing fit she could not control, and, soon, the nun behind her did not hesitate to give her several sharp stinging slaps on her shoulders. Tessa knew that Angela carried things much too far, but found her great fun.

Tessa would never forget one particular day in Sister Monica's class. She and Angela were exchanging notes and giggling over the map of the United States while Sister Monica was pointing out the rivers, the different states, and the physical layout of the country. Tessa and Angela were vying with each other to see who could find the most names of places and titles in the western movies they had seen. They giggled when one of them found Rio Grande, Red River, and Oregon Trail, and the other pointed out the Mississippi River, Dakota, Fargo, Montana, Minnesota, California. It was exciting to see all these names on a real map.

Sister Monica, the geography teacher, was one of the nicest nuns in the school. She never reported or scolded them. Shortly after this particularly lesson, Sister Monica was suddenly transferred to a school on a smaller Caribbean island. She had not been there long when news of a tragedy that had befallen her came back. They were horrified to discover that she had been decapitated. It was a backlash against the whites when independence from Britain was in the air. The students who had loved her grieved for her and for the hate and the racial tension that were being unleashed in the name of Independence.

At the end of the year, Tessa was not promoted with her classmates. When her report card came, she cried bitterly. Sylvia was standing with her on the street outside their house when the mailman handed her the envelope.

"How could they do this to me?" she sobbed as she read what was in it. Sylvia took the report card from her and read it.

"What?" she exclaimed. "You failed English? You who always telling us the teachers read out your essays and stories to the rest of the class, and you always having the right answer in English class when nobody else have it? What is going on? There must be a mistake."

But there was no mistake. Tessa had passed every subject but English, which had been her forte for as long as she could remember. She had always been the best essay writer in her class, even in elementary school. At the age of ten, when she had discovered she could understand the novels of Zane Grey, she was ecstatic that she could read adult books with no trouble. Her male cousins and her brother swapped these western pocket books they bought from the second-hand store. There were no children's books available, but there were lots of Zane Greys around—*The Riders of the Purple Sage, Last of the Plainsmen, The Light of Western Stars, The Lost Wagon Train, West of the Pecos*—all exciting and romantic adventures of the Wild West. After that, she went on to read the Victorian novels her mother and aunts read: *The Rosary, The Woman in White, East Lynne, Ramona, A Death in the Family, The Way of All Flesh*. The City Council had recently opened a branch of the public library in San Juan de la Pina, and Tessa and Sylvia borrowed one novel a week, all that they were allowed, and read them voraciously. They moved on from the Abbey Girls series to read Elizabeth Gouge, A.J. Cronin, Taylor Caldwell, and other popular writers of the time. Once they discovered a writer they liked, they sought out the rest of his or hers books and methodically went through the shelf. All this reading had given Tessa a wide vocabulary and a taste for writing. To lose her year by failing English? The unfairness was heart-rending.

Tessa thought hard and long about why she was being punished. Was it because she had been labelled an idler by fooling around with Angela for most of the year? Sister Aloysius had threatened that she, and not their regular teacher, would mark the English papers for their final exams that year. Sister Aloysius had been enraged when it had been reported by the teachers from St. Francis boys' school across the way that the girls in Tessa's class had been directing mirrors in the midday sun into the boys' classroom, which was across from theirs. "This whole class is a bundle of trouble," Sister Aloysius had ranted. "Your behaviour has been extremely wild and unacceptable. To think that you would have nothing better to do than this, is disgraceful. You will have to be severely punished. For this and for your many other sins, I will be the one to decide who wdill pass and who will fail this year. I will make it my business to mark your English exam papers at the end of the year."

Tessa had not given this threat a second thought. Wasn't she always at the head of her class in English? It was the other subjects she had to worry about. The school never gave out prizes. Her sister and brother always had a prize-giving day at their school. The only time a prize was offered at the Sacred Heart Convent was in commemoration of some important anniversary the Pope was celebrating. Tessa had won the prize for writing the best essay on the Pope, his duties as head of the Roman Catholic Church, his life in the Vatican, and his summer residence at Castel Gandolfo. When she found out that Sister Aloysius had failed her in English while she had passed everything else, she realized something was terribly wrong. She then remembered when she had been summoned to Sister Aloysius's office and what had transpired between them. This meeting had taken place just after the incident about Chinese people and their small mouths.

"Well, Tessa," Sister Aloysius had begun, "I hear you want to know why some nuns take male saints' names, and whether it's because there aren't enough female saints for them to choose from." The nun was snearing at her. It was as though she was saying, "Who are you, a little nobody of a girl to come in here and question our customs?"

Tessa was flabbergasted. Of all the stupid things she had said, that one was so small and unimportant, she wondered why the nun was even bothered by it. Someone had tattled on her, Tessa realized. But who? It couldn't be any of the girls who had been complaining about Sister Marie's remarks about the Chinese people and their small mouths. It must have been someone who had overheard them talking. Tessa suddenly remembered that Darlene O'Meara had been walking behind them. Tessa realized that she should have been more careful, knowing that Darlene was a tattletale, always sucking up to the nuns. Darlene was a "poor white," so she lived, not in St. Elizabeth Park where most of the whites lived, or even in Meadowbrook, which was regarded as a stable middle-class residential area, but in San Juan de la Pina, considered lower middle-class. The O'Mearas' house was a ramshackle one on Main Road. Though the house was not a wooden shack but a concrete bungalow, it had not been painted for a long time and it was surrounded by rum shops, business places, and various vendors. Passersby could see that the O'Mearas' *gallery* was sparsely furnished, without any nice rattan armchairs with stuffed cushions.

One Sunday morning, when Tessa was buying vegetables at the stall where Lucille always sent her, she heard Darlene whispering something to Miss Doreen, the vegetable vendor. Miss Doreen had steupsed. Darlene had been sent by her mother to ask for credit. Miss Doreen was obviously displeased; the O'Mearas probably owed her a lot already. "Alyuh people like to fart low and shit high, if you ask me," Miss Doreen said. Tessa was shocked. She had never heard the expression. And to think that it had been addressed to Darlene, a white girl who attended the convent, shook Tessa to the bone. Tessa was embarrassed for Darlene, and she felt glad that the Joseph family never ran up a bill with the vegetable vendor.

Tessa was dismayed that Sister Aloysius would punish her

in this way for such a small thing. But it was not until many years later that Tessa realized how great an injustice had been done to her. There had been no redress; no one ever challenged exam results or asked to see the corrected exam papers. It had never occurred to Tessa or anyone in her family to confront the nuns. In those days, colour and wealth exerted a powerful influence. The church schools were coveted institutions. For poor people to question the actions of the nuns or priests who ran the schools was to doom your children to expulsion and a life of failure. Tessa's mother would have thought that going to the nuns would only make things worse for Tessa in the remaining years she had to spend there.

Tessa remembered the story that she had overheard Clyde and Manny talking about Simon La Ronde, a boy from their neighbourhood who had been expelled from St. Francis College. Simon had been a bit of a rebel, but he was very smart. In his Higher School Certificate class, he had been enrolled in the language stream. He went into the principal's office to ask Father Emmanuel if he could change to the sciences; he thought that he would have better opportunities in life if he qualified in science rather than languages. Cambridge University divided its studies for the Higher School Certificate into categories of Languages, Modern Studies, Science, and Math. Simon was bilingual as his mother came from the French island of Martinique, so he felt he needed more of a challenge, and he wanted to go into a field of study that would be more useful to him in later life. When Father Emmanuel refused his request, Simon lost his temper. He told Clyde and Manny he didn't know why or where the terrible swear words he used that day came from. They just slipped out. He was promptly expelled. Before he got home on his bicycle, his mother had already been telephoned. Simon was sent by his family to England to finish his studies.

England turned out to be a refuge for many young men and women for various reasons. Agatha Samuels, a young woman the family knew, had been studying at the Teachers' Training

College, where the students were expected to board for their two years of study. There were strict curfews, and she had broken one of those. She had been in an accident, and her story had been splashed on the front pages of the newspapers. She, too, was promptly expelled in disgrace. She went to England and studied nursing. Another boy in San Juan de la Pina attending Our Lady of Lourdes College had fatally shot a neighbourhood boy with his father's hunting rifle. After avoiding the noose, for his wealthy father hired the best criminal lawyer on the island, he, too escaped to England to finish his high school studies. Then there was Peter, a neighbour's boy who was a brilliant mathematician. Because he hadn't passed the compulsory English paper in the Senior Cambridge exam, he was be granted a third grade certificate. To enter the Civil Service, you had to have either a first or second grade certificate. Peter pursued university education in England, where he succeeded in obtaining a degree in mathematics. He returned to the island and became famous for tutoring hundreds of students who were having difficulty in math in high school and helped them to pass their exams. It seemed that England, the mother country, solved many educational problems for its colonial subjects in the 1950s. Of course, only for those who could afford to do so.

However, England was not a haven for everyone. Tessa heard Lucille and Clyde talking about Timothy Miller, a young man whose parents Lucille had known from childhood in the village of de Gannes. After many years of working and studying in England, Timothy Miller had returned with a Bachelor's degree that entitled him to employment at the prestigious Our Lady of Lourdes College, where Clyde went to school. As a Black man in England in the fifties, he had faced his share of discrimination and prejudice. These incidents had rendered him bitter and suspicious, and he passed this on to the students he was hired to teach. They began to hate him and to reciprocate his unpleasant behaviour by being as difficult as they could be, baiting him and playing tricks on him. Timothy's reputation preceded him. It was rumoured that he had written letters to the Queen, protesting his Third Class degree, letters to which he had never received a reply. On his return to the island, he dressed in a black suit and tie and a bowler hat, and he carried an umbrella. He walked long distances, so he became well known in many parts of the city. Wearing this English style of dress in the tropical heat, inevitably labelled him as eccentric or "mad"—the most commonly used to describe him.

At the beginning of the next term, Tessa discovered that Angela had left the school. Her father had been transferred by his bank to Barbados and she would now attend the expensive and prestigious boarding school, St. Ursuline's Convent. Tessa never heard from her again, and she felt betrayed. Tessa's failure that year meant that she had lost the chance to be accepted into the accelerated four-year program with her class. How silly she had been wasting time with Angela. Now she would pay the price. Angela, she knew, would not suffer. She didn't need much education to get a job, not with her father's position at the bank.

It was then that Tessa understood one of the maxims her mother and the older islanders frequently threw around. People should stay with their own kind. She did not belong with people like Angela. The Black grandmother in the movie *Pinky* warned her half-white granddaughter in the American south, who "passed for white," to "stay in your own backyard." Among the hundreds of down-to-earth folk sayings the islanders used was the expression, "Cockroach don't belong in fowl party." Being with people of a higher class than yourself left you open not only to hurt and humiliation, but also to social destruction. When people like Angela became friends with you, they were only patronizing you, and like the cockroach in the fowl party, you will only be eaten up.

15.
New Friends

THE PHILOSOPHERS and the elders say that all life experiences, even the bad ones, have a purpose. Or they say that God has a hand in it all. Or that life's events form a pattern on a quilt that will only be completed at the end of the journey. The Greeks believed in a fate that was pre-ordained, no matter how hard one tried to avoid it. Caribbean Nobel Laureate Derek Walcott says that talk of an afterlife after a death means little to the mourners: *"Is like telling mourners round the graveside about resurrection, they want the dead back."*

Though Tessa was not in the accelerated four-year program with her class, some consolations emerged. Two new girls, Rosanna De Aguilar and Ashley Summers, moved into the neighbourhood and were now registered in her class. Rosanna lived two doors down from the Joseph family, and Ashley lived in a house on Silk Cotton Road, around the corner from Victory Street.

Rosanna's mother was Venezuelan, and her late father was a white Trinidadian. She had an older sister, Manuela, who worked in an office downtown.

Every Friday night, the De Aguilars, accompanied by a young man from the neighbourhood who was courting Manuela, would stop at the Joseph house on their way to the cinema. Senora De Aguilar was chaperoning her daughter in true Spanish style.

One Friday, as the two older women sat in the drawing room

while the young people were in the *gallery*—Mrs. De Aguilar confided her life story to Lucille, who later relayed it to Tessa and Sylvia.

"You know, my mother and father was gypsies. I born in Romania. And we come to Venezuela. I was dancer. I meet Leo in Caracas. The family don't want him to marry me. After we get married we come here to live. His family don't have nothing to do with us. You know the De Aguilars—they important people in the island, but they never let us come to their big house, all the years I married to him. But Leo was good doctor. He didn't ask them for anything after we get married. But now, is not so easy, we don't have money as before. I think when my girls get older I take them back to Venezuela. They could get good jobs, make lots of money, with all the oil fields over there."

Senora De Aguilar wore heavy makeup, always dressed in black widow's weeds, wore high-heeled shoes and lots of jewellery, including long, dangling earrings or huge hoop earrings. She chain-smoked and coughed continuously. Lucille, who would never have dreamed of putting a cigarette to her lips— that was a strictly male habit—suggested to Mrs. De Aguilar, "Perhaps it's the cigarettes that make you cough so much."

"No, no, no, I don't think so," she said. "Cigarettes don't make you cough."

Rosanna and Manuela brought a glimpse of another lifestyle to Tessa and Sylvia. The De Aguilars's house was filled with numerous books and magazines. Tessa and Sylvia borrowed the English women's magazines that the De Aguilars subscribed to, *Women's Weekly* and *Women's Day*. They feasted on the romantic stories featured every week—stories set in African colonies, where the white overseers had romantic liaisons with visiting English women, or stories of women in suburban England—opening up worlds so different from their own. Though the De Aguilars's house was only slightly larger than Tessa's, it was furnished in a much better style. It was kept in such good order that Tessa vowed that one day, she too would live in such surroundings. Not the way their family lived, never having enough room to put everything in its place, but in a house as dignified and as well run as the De Aguilars's.

Manuela, Rosanna's sister, was a great reader, and Tessa showed her some of the stories and poems she had written. Manuela, not knowing anyone else of Tessa's age who aspired to be a writer and who was trying to hone such a skill, declared that Tessa's writing was very good. Tessa, like Jane Austen, hid her writing from prying eyes. Only Sylvia knew of her writing ambitions, and only Manuela was allowed to see her first drafts. When Tessa was writing a poem for the Aunt Juanita's contest in the local paper, the *Trinidad Guardian*, it was Manuela who helped her polish it and encouraged her to submit it. The poem was to commemorate the Coronation of Queen Elizabeth II.

The Sunday morning when her name appeared in the children's section of the newspaper as the first-prize winner, Manuela came over to congratulate her. It was nine o'clock, and the Joseph family was just back from their six-thirty Mass.

Manuela held out her hand to Tessa. "Congratulations," she said warmly.

Tessa was overwhelmed. A grown-up congratulating her and shaking her hand. She suddenly felt shy and disoriented.

"Thank you," she whispered, "for all your help."

"No, you wrote the poem. I hardly changed anything in it. It's a good poem. You deserve first prize."

The whole family was thrilled. The prize was a book, *Treasure Island*, by Robert Louis Stevenson.

Rosanna was a good friend to have fun with and her sister's generosity was a godsend to Tessa. But Rosanna was not very interested in studying; she always found more exciting things to do: roller skating, hanging out, or *liming* with the boys on the corner. Lucille Joseph did not allow her daughters to *lime* on the corner, especially with any group that included boys. Lucille often wondered out loud why Mrs. De Aguilar allowed

Rosanna such freedom, while she made sure to chaperone Manuela every Friday night when Manuela went to the movies with her boyfriend. So Tessa kept her nose to the grindstone where her studies were concerned, especially after the dismal loss of her year. There was nothing else to do, and there was hardly ever any money for anything anyway. A cheap cinema show in the neighbourhood second-run cinema, which was in walking distance, was the only treat that their mother could manage once or twice a month.

Manuela had recently got her driver's licence, and she would include the two sisters whenever she, Rosanna, and their mother spent a day at the beach or went for drives in the country.

In spite of her bitter disappointment at the loss of a year, Tessa remained loyal to her convent school, defending it and the nuns whenever anyone dared to criticize either. For Tessa, the school was a beacon of peace, quiet, order, and gentility in a world that was quarrelsome, noisy, chaotic, and often uncivilized. It offered her gentility and civilized behaviour. Tessa thought that only rich white people knew what these qualities were, for they were the only ones who did not live in the demeaning circumstances of most of the islanders.

Years later, when Tessa returned to the school as an invited guest, she saw that it was as dignified and well run as before. However, she noticed that two major changes. For one, there was a conspicuous absence of the white-clothed figures. In the 1990s, the Sacred Heart Order of Nuns was sadly lacking in new recruits. But the school still boasted the same hallowed halls of learning, carrying the weight of the long past behind them, and it still oozed tradition and serenity. The elegant mahogany staircase—which was always out of bounds to students and led to the nuns' parlour on one side and the teachers' staff room on the other—was as imposing and as highly polished as ever. In a world in which so much had changed, this stability was a source of amazement to Tessa. The other stark difference was the racial composition of the school's population. There were few white girls. Most of the students were light coloured or Black, and all of them were steeped in quiet self-confidence. There were few East Indians as by that time the Presbyterians and Hindus had opened their own schools and their girls no longer had to travel the long distances from the country to the capital in order to obtain a high school education, only to be discriminated against by all the other races. The Hindu and Presbyterian schools were now mainly populated with their own kind, and with any non-Indians from the district who had won places in the eleven-plus exam and had chosen the neighbourhood schools as their schools of choice rather than the schools in Port of Spain. A free education for all policy had been instituted by the newly-elected independent government of the island and thus school doors were wide open to everyone. The eleven-plus exam, adopted after Britain had already discarded it and now called the SEA exam, put the children through rigorous tests in English and Mathematics, and those who placed in the first five hundred secured places in their first school of choice. These were the prestigious colleges and convents. The students who obtained these places were inevitably the ones whose parents had put them through rigorous after school and weekend classes and who had the time, money, and access to transportation to do so. It meant that the class system was being perpetuated under the education banner. The children of the white population were now attending the expensive and private Maple Leaf Canadian School or the International School, which ensured their admission into Canadian and other universities around the world.

Tessa, Sylvia, Rosanna, and Ashley soon coalesced into a firm group. After cajoling and harassing her mother for months, Tessa had recently gotten a bike, A family friend had told them of a fairly new second-hand bike that they could purchase at a reasonable price. Tessa and her new friends rode their bikes to school together and went to the cinema on Sunday afternoons. Sylvia had friends of her own from school as well, but somehow the Joseph's house was filled with Tessa's friends or the Joseph's relatives.

The group decided to put on a play for the annual church concert. Since it was Tessa's idea, she had to find a suitable play from the neighbourhood library. She assumed single-handedly the roles of director, costume mistress, and stage manager. She was advised and guided in all this by Manuela. Although the De Aguilars were not churchgoers, Manuela could never keep away from anything that smacked of creativity. The play, *The Spinsters of Lushe*, had enough roles for everyone. Ashley, who was slim, tall, and elegant, had the starring role of Miss Lucy. The others were gossiping spinsters whose job it was to "bad talk" Miss Lucy, the youngest and most beautiful among them.

Months before the play, Tessa badgered all their relatives and neighbours for old dresses and shoes for the actresses to wear. Hats, however, were a problem as most women in Trinidad had given up the hat-wearing custom of previous eras. And since the Pope had rescinded the law on head coverings for women, Catholic women were now going to church hatless. Hats were considered one more expense they could do without.

Tessa finally thought of Dolores, their dressmaker. Women like Dolores who belonged to the fundamentalist churches, often predominantly Black churches, still wore hats to church. Dolores lent Tessa some hats that Tessa knew that Lucille would certainly denounce as "*coskell*." This was a word used to describe clothes that were too showy, earrings that were too large, or hats that were too lavishly decorated. Dolores' hats were adorned with flowers and fruit, and Tessa thought they looked authentic enough to pass as early-twentieth-century English-style hats.

The actresses learned their lines while Tessa assembled appropriate props and scheduled a dress rehearsal in the Joseph's miniscule drawing room. Tessa felt sure she had not forgotten anything. The play was bound to be a roaring success. They would all be stars and the director the biggest star of all. She had never, in all her complex preparations and hours of hard work, anticipated what was going to happen.

The day of the dress rehearsal, Rosanna startled them all by throwing a crying fit.

"I'm not going to wear this ratty old dress," she wept.

The long dress had been somebody's mother's wedding dress and was quite a mess. It was yellowed with age, the lace was ripped in places, and the hem was dirty.

Sylvia whispered to Tessa under her breath. "She's right. I wouldn't wear that dress either. It looks terrible."

She giggled while Tessa floundered, wondering how on earth she would fix this crisis.

The others crowded around Rosanna. "It's all right, Rosanna. It doesn't look too bad," Ashley soothed her.

"Come on, Rosanna," Tessa said, trying hard not to ask her why she was being such a damn fool and, at the same time, wondering if all her hard work was going down the drain like dirty dishwater. "It will only be for a few minutes. It's not for long."

At that moment, Manuela stopped by the house to see how they were getting along. "Rosanna," she scolded her sister. "Where do you think we can find another dress for you at this late hour? The concert is tomorrow, remember? Be a sport, and I'll take everybody for ice cream sundaes at Kong Chow Café after the concert."

That was all Rosanna needed. Ice cream sundaes at Kong Chow was a treat like no other. The sundaes always consisted of three scoops of ice cream in real ice cream glasses, smothered in chocolate sauce, sprinkled with cherries and chopped nuts, and garnished with flakes of coconut. Tessa was to discover that no ice cream concoction she would enjoy in different parts of the world—no banana split, Italian cassata, or spumoni—could match the flavour of Kong Chow's coconut ice cream sundaes.

In later years, Tessa often wondered whether the night of the play had taught her anything. She was constantly bashing her head against the proverbial brick wall, striving to achieve what everyone said was impossible. At times she badgered herself mercilessly. Why did she never learn from past mistakes? She would be carried away by some wild scheme, trying to reach a goal that nobody else would have dreamed of aspiring to. She wondered if she was always tilting at windmills like Don Quixote. But then she heard Browning's words—"Ah, but a man's reach should exceed his grasp, or what's a Heaven for?"—and she would continue on her restless quests.

The night of the play, no one forgot her lines, everyone entered on cue, and the girls looked and behaved like proper English spinsters in a respectable drawing room in an English village. But two basic tenets of dramatic presentation were unfortunately lacking. The first was that San Juan de la Pina Girls' School, a simple one-room school building, was a far cry from a proper theatre with a sloping floor. What transpired on the stage was visible only to those at the front of the hall. The second was that the performers knew nothing of voice projection. The only people who laughed heartily in the appropriate places were the nuns and priests who sat in the first few rows. They were the only ones who could hear.

16.
Austen, Marrying Well, and Tragedy in the Neighbourhood

IN TESSA'S FIFTH-FORM year, Jane Austen's *Northanger Abbey* was the literary text chosen for the English Literature Cambridge Senior School Certificate examination for her class. Mrs. Maloney, their teacher, had explained that Jane Austen never wrote love scenes. When the class got to the end of the book, Tessa decided that the ending was too flat—it needed a romantic love scene. She proceeded to write one in the style of the romance novels and the English magazine stories she had been devouring.

Tessa thought that the scene in which Henry Tilney defies his father's snobbery and travels a great distance to declare his love for Catherine Morland was not thrilling enough. It did no justice to the hero, who, Tessa decided, was one of the nicest men any writer had depicted in nineteenth-century English literature. Austen had merely written, in the final scene between Henry Tilney and Catherine: "She was assured of his affection: and that heart in return was solicited, which perhaps, they pretty equally knew was his own...."

Utterly inadequate, Tessa thought. Though Catherine was genuine and good-natured, a complete contrast to her friend Isabella—one of those shallow, rattling women Austen was so good at creating—Catherine was nevertheless a rather naive and untalented heroine. But Catherine certainly deserved better than this, thought Tessa.

So, Tessa wrote:

Henry Tilney took her hand and pressed it to his lips, saying, "O, Catherine, my dear Catherine, how you have suffered at the hands of my father. I intend to make it up to you." Catherine, of course, did not withdraw her hand, but only blushed furiously, enjoying the pressure of his warm and comforting hand in her small one and his lips upon it. In the next moment Henry Tilney was enclosing her in his arms, and whispering against her cheek all the phrases a woman in love wants to hear. Catherine was explaining in return how miserable she had been since her return from Northanger Abbey, not having been able to say goodbye to him, puzzled as to what she had done to incur the General's displeasure, and fearing that because of the General she was never to see Henry Tilney again. It was no time for words, however. She was soon silenced with his warm loving lips upon hers, and all General Tilney's cruelty faded into the background.

Mrs. Maloney, one of the few lay teachers at the school, left her desk and came over to see what was causing the giggles. Tessa was made to hand over what she had written. Everyone sat in agony. What would Mrs. Maloney say? Or do? Would Tessa have to face Sister Aloysius? There was already enough discord between them. Tessa had heard that Sister Aloysius was reputed to have some East Indian ancestry, and her colour was certainly not very white, but that had not stopped her from harassing Tessa, who was one of the only twenty or so Indian girls at a school of six hundred.

Mrs. Maloney laughed out loud. "Well done, Tessa," she said approvingly. "Daring to improve on Jane Austen's writing. You have some spunk, I must say."

The girls, sitting quietly and quaking in fear, could not believe Mrs. Maloney's reaction. Was it because she was not a nun? And that she was a married woman? That was the end of the incident. It was never reported to the principal.

In the long July-August vacation, when the wealthy girls at the convent retreated to their beach houses or went on tours to England, France, or America with their parents, Tessa found time heavy on her hands. Even Rosanna and Ashley went away. Tessa was glad that she had a bike, which gave her freedom to leave the confines of the house. She would ride to the Central Library near the Queen's Park Savannah, in the posh residential district of the old ruling class. This library had been given to the island by the Americans and was more lavishly stocked than the Public Library. Since the Public Library was downtown, it was a more dangerous route to navigate by bike. At the Central Library, Tessa borrowed the other five Austen novels, and spent her vacation days and nights absorbing them. To her delight, she discovered books of criticism devoted to Austen's craft. Her mind was suffused with sharp and intricate discussions by rival critics of the merits, characters, and themes of each book. They all agreed on one thing, however: in wit and irony, in gracefulness of prose, Austen had no rival. Tessa could not get enough of these books. The critics argued their points of view ferociously, contradicting each other's theories in sometimes insulting and witty put-downs. She began to imagine herself on an equal footing with these critics. Yet there was no one with whom she could share all this until her English Honours class at university. When Austen became popular in the 1990s, and her novels were adapted into films, Tessa regarded all Austen's fans with pity. For hadn't they been deprived all these years of the joys of Austen, which she had enjoyed for so long?

Tessa, thoroughly imbued with the language of Jane Austen's society, found herself examining her own social milieu and concluded that there was no difference between the society of Jane Austen's England and that of the East Indian people in Trinidad. In Austen's world, a woman's chances of "marrying well" depended heavily on the size of her fortune. In the East

Indian society in Trinidad, the girls' parents offered a dowry. In both cases the women are being sold, Tessa thought.

A phrase from Austen's books, "to marry well," was also used by her aunts and mother, but Tessa puzzled over what exactly the phrase meant in Trinidad, so far removed from Austen's England. She began to listen to the aunts more closely when they whispered or "shoo-shooed" with her mother on their evening visits. They seldom came all together, only whenever they found some time from their numerous and confining household tasks. Tessa finally deduced that "to marry well" meant marrying a man who was a civil servant or a teacher. Partnering with anyone who worked as a labourer, a farmer, or a taxi driver was out of the question. But Tessa began to see how closed their own society was. Was it any larger than Austen's "two or three families in a country village?" Contemplating her own society, Tessa realized that the Josephs' social circles consisted of the extended family and their church community, which included people of all races, but mostly consisted of the Black and mixed-race people of the middle and lower classes. This posed a problem for the young people when it came to choosing who their parents would consider suitable marriage partners, particularly if the parents insisted that their children should marry only within their own race.

Clyde, as usual, theorized about this dilemma. He concluded that the Josephs and their relatives who lived in San Juan de la Pina did not really belong anywhere, being Indian and Catholic in a city in which they were a minority.

One day, as the family was sitting in the drawing room and the question of marrying your own kind came up, Clyde said, "I wish our family was Presbyterian and not Catholic. Because the Presbyterians are all East Indians, their boys and girls marry each other. When the Canadian Mission Church went into the East Indian villages to convert the people, they opened schools for them as well. When asked by the government why the Indians needed their own schools, why they couldn't go to the government schools, the Canadian Missionary, I think his name was Morton, explained that the East Indian would not allow his child to go to the mixed-race school. He was afraid the Creole teacher would be unfair to his children and the Creole pupils would treat them badly. I read that in a book in the library just the other day. And because of their education, the Presbyterians have more advantages than people like us. So many of them went on to attend universities in Canada and England and became doctors and engineers. But how many educated Indian families in San Juan de la Pina do we have to associate with? Most of them are Moslem or Hindu, and they socialize among their own people. Besides, their parents always arrange marriages for them. But our family laughs at the idea of arranged marriages. But there are so few families who are Catholic and Indian. And if any of us decide to marry a non-Indian, we only asking for trouble."

"Is not only because they were Presbyterians that they became doctors and engineers," Sylvia remarked. "Don't forget those people in the south have lots of money, oil money. We don't have any money to go away to university, Catholic or not."

Clyde and his sisters knew that although their immediate and extended family always taught their children to respect people of all races, never to make racial slurs, or to use the dreaded N-word, and to accept friends of all races with warmth and hospitality, they still expected their children to marry people of their own race.

"Marrying outside the race is never a good thing," Lucille Joseph had warned. "It creates too much confusion; it's not really worth it," they heard her say often enough. "Look at Aunt Josephine," she would say. "She went and married that half-white man, that Harold Sebastian, even though everyone had warned her against him. He was an illegitimate child from our village. His father, Eugene, was one of the children of the white estate owner. He was the wild son, and went around having children with women of all races. His white relatives used to keep him away from their houses because of his reputation. And also because the French-Creole family would not accept any relative who was not pure white. Harold Sebastian's mother was an Indian girl from our village. One of those stupid women who didn't understand that the white man would never marry her—he only wanted one thing." Lucille Joseph would never use the word "sex," but that's what she meant.

She continued, "When Josephine was first married to Harold Sebastian, she had a nice life, going to balls at the Princes Building, dressing up in fancy ball gowns—something none of us ever had a chance to do. But that only lasted until the war came."

"So what happened when the war came?" Tessa asked.

"He couldn't get the materials for his factory. The Germans were all over the seas—even in the Caribbean—and bombing ships left right and centre. His business failed, and he began to drink. And, you know how he is still a senseless drunk."

None of Lucille's other sisters had husbands who were drunks. They were sober and hard-working men, stern of demeanour and strictly homebodies. They were never in rum shops drinking with the boys like so many of the island men. When Harold Sebastian went on the rampage, Josephine would flee in the middle of the night with her four children and come to the Josephs' house. Tessa often wondered why her mother felt she had an obligation to take her in. Josephine was an "outside" child of Lucille's father, Gopinath Samnaddan-Pillai. His wife Lakshmi had raised her husband's child since Josephine's own mother was a free spirit who refused to be tied down. It was a simpler time. Tessa and Sylvia had always called her "Aunt Josephine."

Lucille's sisters all advised Josephine to leave her husband, though where she would go and how she would support herself and her four children was anybody's guess. Eventually, when she felt it had blown over, Josephine would go back to her husband and the cycle would be repeated. Even the parish priest had once said to Josephine, "Woman, where you going with your four children?"

On one visit, Aunt Josephine brought a large wooden trunk to the Josephs' house. One morning, when their mother and aunt were away, Tessa and Sylvia opened the trunk to investigate its contents. It was filled with luxuries they had seen only in the movies. There were long, stunning ball gowns of lace and satin; dance programs; beaded evening bags and fans; and sling-backed, high-heeled evening sandals encrusted with stones.

"So it's true," Tessa whispered, awed by everything that was in the trunk; it was like something out of a fairy tale. "She lived a fancy life, nothing like those lives our mother and aunts had. All they did was go to church and stay at home and keep house, sew and cook and look after children. Imagine Aunt Josephine wearing all this stuff."

"And now she's nothing but a pauper," Sylvia added. "And the only place she can come to is ours, because we have no man in the house. You think any of the other uncles would let their wives take her and her children in? Never happen."

"When you see how Aunt Josephine have to suffer after she take up with a man like Harold Sebastian is one good reason not to get involved with anyone outside the race," the aunts and Lucille Joseph warned their children.

Sometimes, when he was quietly savouring the numbing effects of his drunkenness, and had no energy left to physically abuse his family, Harold Sebastian would swear and cuss Josephine and his children in a low monologue. One day, their cousin Camille was visiting that miserable household and she heard him say, "the *coolie* asshole," over and over again in his drunken state, and later told Tessa and Sylvia about it. Their mother of course, would never have told them of anything so abominable. And so Tessa and her cousins began to believe that Harold Sebastian was indeed the living example of the danger of "taking up" with someone from another race.

The extended family believed, as did many people on the island, that Indians knew how to live frugally. Everyone said that the Indians never spent their money on fêtes and fancy clothes like the people of the other races. Those other people belonged to a "Carnival culture," spending thousands on Carnival costumes and going to fêtes every weekend, not only at Carnival time.

Tessa often wondered why people would say that the Indians were more frugal than the other races. What evidence of frugal living was there among her immediate or extended family? It was true that none of them took part in Carnival, but they all had to have new cushions for the Morris chairs and new curtains for their windows every Christmas. They felt obliged to stock their kitchens with Christmas cake called *"black cake,"* which was heavily laden with minced prunes, raisins, currants, and nuts, then laced with rum and cherry brandy, and made black by adding a syrup of burnt brown sugar and water. They would buy chocolates and English biscuits to be served when relatives and neighbours came for Christmas visits. Not to do so would be considered shameful. It all cost money. They also spent money on new clothes for to wear to church and family weddings. Where was the frugal living?

The Joseph family had adopted western culture and all that it entailed. They were not like the Indians in the country who still lived in huts plastered with dung and mud, and were so self-sufficient that they did not have to depend on store-bought foods. These country people felt no social obligation to decorate their houses or to entertain their neighbours at Christmas. They had their own celebrations, *pujas* and elaborate feasts for weddings, births, and *Diwali*, the festival of lights. Every Hindu household lit up small clay lamps called *deyas* and placed them outside their huts or houses on Diwali nights. Their food, however, was cheap, since they cooked no meat at these festivities. And their everyday meals were *roti* and *dahl* and lentils and beans. They ate the numerous root vegetables that abounded in the island. They cooked green bananas in ingenious ways and fried the ripe plantains. They grew many varieties of green vegetables, and their yards often had avocado and breadfruit trees. The heavy, large breadfruit yielded a nutritious starchy vegetable that could sustain a family for a week, if necessary. They had cows and goats that gave them milk and meat. In lieu of passage money back to India, the Indian indentured labourers had been offered five acres of land by the British after their five-year contracts had been fulfilled. So many of them prospered by working the fertile plains of the island, or cultivating rice in the swampland they had been given, on lands no one else thought had any value.

But Tessa often wondered how come so few of her relatives had any land. Did they sell it? Did they leave it in favour of a life in the city? She knew so little of her grandparents, on both sides. Both groups had come so long ago that no one was able to trace their roots.

So what did people mean by saying that Indians knew how to save and were not extravagant? Tessa wondered. They must be referring to the Indians in the country, not Indians like themselves who lived in San Juan de la Pina. And as for telling your children not to marry outside the race, wasn't that being racist? Or prejudiced? Yet everyone in the island was prejudiced against everyone else, Tessa reflected. Except for Rosanna, her close friends were all of mixed-race—"red-skin" people as they were known in the island. At the convent, the girls with French, Spanish, and English names of historical significance in the island, made sure everyone knew how important they were. Many of them, however, were mixed with Black blood and were only the "outside branch" of the illustrious families. Basically, girls like Tessa were ignored. Yet some of the white girls of truly aristocratic families, either French or English, were the least snobbish. When it was the turn of the Joseph family to receive the statue of our Lady of

Fatima in their home, as it made its island-wide tour, Tessa asked Jean, one of the girls whose home she rode past every day in St. Elizabeth Park, if she could get a few of the beautiful roses she saw in their garden. Being good Catholics and knowing the significance of the occasion, Jean's family did not refuse. They gave her huge bunches of the full-blown roses. Then there was Simone, from one of the old French Creole families. Simone helped her in the kitchen when Tessa was deathly afraid of lighting the gas stove.

Recently, however, frightening rumours had begun to circulate regarding race and politics. Some of the newly-elected Black Caribbean governments were practising racism against the East Indians. The acts of violence against many East Indian communities in Guyana had caused many East Indians to flee to Canada. And in Trinidad, the Black government was initiating policies that would move the Blacks into the agricultural enclaves that had historically been populated by the Indians. There was a move afoot to *"douglarize"* the race, to make the Blacks and Indians, if not marry, at least breed. And the rumours abounded that the new party that had recently been elected, led by a Black intellectual, would only look after the concerns and issues of the Black people. The East Indians, the Prime Minister had said, "were a recalcitrant minority." The new government would not have much use for the mulattoes either. The "high brown" people who had been next on the social rung after the whites no longer counted, it seemed.

But though these rumours troubled Tessa, as it did so many who were not Black, she began to wonder why the people of the island put people of different races into little boxes. Indians are frugal and have strong family values; Blacks like to fête and do not have stable family lives; whites have all the power and money; Chinese and Portuguese people make good shopkeepers; Syrian people sell cloth. How did the eight relatives of their widowed cousin Dularie show any family values when they moved into her neat concrete bungalow, crowding her out and sending her on the path to a nervous breakdown? Dularie would come to the Joseph's house begging a ten-cent or twenty-five cent piece. Lucille Joseph, after handing over the money, would be livid, and would say, after Dularie left, "What a shame! I don't know why she has to come and beg like this! After who she was."

"Who was she?" Sylvia asked. "You always say that every time she comes here begging for money."

Lucille explained that Dularie was the only daughter of one of the richest men in their village. She had had an extravagant wedding, and was even carried in *a palanquin* on the day of the wedding.

"What's a *palanquin?*" Tessa asked.

"It's a tent covered in silk with long poles in which the bride is carried to the wedding celebration and to the bridegroom's house." The wedding party going to the bridegroom's house is a necessary part of the Hindu ritual.

"So her father had lots of money. None of you were ever married in a *palanquin*, were you?" Sylvia asked.

"No, not us. We were married in church in white wedding dresses, not in *saris* or Indian clothes. Except for our first two sisters. But I don't think they were carried in *palanquins.*"

"But why did her husband's relatives all move into Dularie's house after her husband died?" asked Tessa.

"That is the custom of Indian people—a widow is nothing. So they thought they would take everything she had, once her husband was dead. They were supposed to be helping her, but so many of them? Eating her out of house and home, that's what it is, and sending her to the madhouse soon, if you ask me," Lucille Joseph explained.

"Some custom Indian people have," said Tessa scornfully. "They should be ashamed of themselves. Look at Uncle Solomon. He hires all his nephews in his business and pays them starvation wages. And they all living in shacks, and they can't afford to send their children to high school, or buy bikes for them while he residing in splendour in St. Elizabeth Park, and driving a long black American limousine. Indian people greedy for money, if you ask me," said Tessa.

"Indian people not more greedy than anybody else, you will find out, girl," scolded Lucille. "That is human nature. As you get older you will find that greedy people come from every race and every class. Who always help when we have trouble? The neighbours, no matter what race they are."

Lucille Joseph was right. One day there was trouble, trouble like they had never seen before, and hoped never to see again.

The family was returning from a day in St. Louisburg, in the south of the island. Their cousin Selwyn had just graduated as a doctor, and had taken up an appointment in the hospital there. It was Selwyn who had been supported emotionally by Lucille Joseph when his father had thrown him out of the house for "riotous living" all those years ago. Selwyn had somehow been able to shake off the yoke of his brothel-running wife and had gone away to study. After graduation he had secured this prestigious job in St. Louisburg, and he wanted his aunt who had been good to him to share in his celebration. He had sent a chauffeured car for them early in the day.

They returned at six o'clock that night to a scene of horror. The blood-curdling screams coming from next door were eerily like the ones that the Joseph family had experienced during their visit to Darling in Cocorico. This time they heard not only screams, but also noises of furniture crashing and someone shouting curses and threats. Clyde and Lucille, having given strict instructions to the two girls to stay where they were, and not even think of following them, were rushing over to the Blackmans' house, not knowing what they would find. Mrs. Meredith, from the house next door to the Blackmans', was already there. A big woman, she was grappling with Mr. Blackman, trying to wrest a bloody knife from his hands. He had been hacking at his wife when Mrs.

Meredith, hearing the screams, rushed into the house and, with no fear for her own life, heroically began tried to stop him. When Clyde and Lucille arrived, as they told the girls later, they saw him slump to the ground as if in a daze. Mrs. Meredith, a large strong woman, had overpowered this small man. Mr. Blackman was a butcher by trade, and the knife was one of gleaming steel.

Soon a crowd gathered around the house where the tragedy had taken place, and a number of police cars arrived. Police? Crowds? This was not their quiet peaceful neighbourhood. The day had already been so eventful. Driving in a chauffeured car, being entertained lavishly in an old colonial house, which would have been occupied only by white doctors in the past and was now the home of their cousin Selwyn. And to return to this? It was all too much for one day.

Their cousins from the next street were standing among the crowd. "Mr. Blackman went mad and attacked his wife. With his butcher knife. I would never have believed anything like that could happen in this neighbourhood. We don't live in any slum. We not behind the bridge," Sherry told Tessa and Sylvia. The east end of the city was a notoriously violent area.

"Went mad? Mr. Blackman?"

Why? Tessa thought. He was the mildest, most conscientious husband and father to be found, on this street and anywhere else. He had often invited Tessa and Sylvia to go to the beach with his family, since the Josephs had no car, and there was no way of getting to the beach without a car. He was at home with his family every evening, mowed his lawn, kept beautiful flowers, and did chores around the house and yard. In fact, he was a model husband and father. Tessa, standing there listening to what the neighbours were saying, began to feel the familiar sick feeling welling up into her throat from the pit of her stomach. The feeling that always overcame her when anything bad happened. If this could happen here, in this street, if a man like Mr. Blackman could do a thing like this—a man who never was out boozing with the boys after work or on weekends, who did not have an "outside woman" like so many island men—then nothing was impossible in this world. Nothing was certain. Outward signs of respectability were not to be trusted. Middle-class respectability was no guarantee of safety and sanity.

For it had to be insanity.

The screams from the house had caused Mrs. Meredith to come running from next door to see what could be happening in this house, which was always quiet, in which there had never been any fights, or quarrels between husband and wife. The children were never beaten either.

Mr. Blackman was taken away to jail. At the trial that followed, the verdict was insanity, and he was sent to the mental hospital instead of serving time in jail. The story that was passed around claimed that his job at one of the most successful businesses in the town was to be terminated. This, it seemed, had sent him over the edge.

Mrs. Warren, the neighbour on the other side, told Tessa and Sylvia, "You know that he didn't have a job anymore? You heard what happened? Mr. Beacon, the man who started the big grocery store and then opened a chain of grocery stores, decided to retire. He sold the business to somebody from the States, and the new owner don't care about people like Mr. Blackman. People with children, men who started there as lil' boys of seventeen and worked their way up to be managers and bosses."

Someone else said, "You heard he was buying a bigger house? He was going to move in as soon as he sold this one. And now, this blow came. He couldn't take it. His mind went. And this is what he do to his poor wife, who didn't have anything to do with it."

Tessa and Sylvia could only stare at the Blackman house. They thought about the many hours they had spent at that house. They had been there so many times for children's parties and on Sunday afternoons for coconut ice cream. They had helped to churn the ice cream on the hand-cranked ice cream freezer. They stared sadly at the house barricaded with yellow police tape.

Relatives soon came and took away the now motherless children.

17.
Marriage by Letter

THE JOSEPH FAMILY was attending the wedding of Uncle Lou and Aunt Millicent's eldest daughter. It was an elaborate church wedding. The bride's dress was in the latest fashion, and her six bridesmaids were dressed in satin, three in blue, and three in pink with large floppy hats in matching colours. Their gloves and shoes, their bouquets of hydrangeas, all matched the colours of their dresses. All the men in the bridal party as well as the guests wore heavy, dark, English suits despite the heat of the tropical afternoon.

The ceremony, at four o'clock on a Saturday afternoon, was formal and solemn. The men were seated on one side of the church, the women on the other. Tessa and Sylvia wondered about this custom. Before the wedding, they had heard the adults pairing off the girls and boys of each side according to their ideas of suitability. Why split them up at the church?

Tessa and Sylvia were both too young to be given escorts, and as Clyde was still in school, he was not eligible. Anyway, the two girls reasoned, splitting up the couples was only for the church part of the wedding; these paired off young people would meet later at the reception. Tessa heard Aunt Clarissa complaining about the boy who had been sent for her daughter, saying, "What they mean by sending that Regis boy as my daughter's escort? I don't like that family at all. They are good-for-nothing wastrels, low-class people. I will have to tell Millicent to make sure the bridegroom find somebody else for my daughter. I won't allow it. I don't want my daughter paired off with that boy."

And after all the fuss, about who was suitable and who wasn't, why they split everybody up at the church was a question to which nobody could give a reasonable answer. Tessa and Sylvia both agreed, however, that the entire wedding was very elegant and colourful—a break in everyone's drab and hard-working lives. Their Aunt Violet, the youngest of Lakshmi and Gopinath's children—who had taken singing and piano lessons, a luxury none of the others had ever enjoyed—sang Gounod's "Ave Maria" at the church ceremony, and everyone marvelled at her accomplished singing voice.

The wedding reception was held outside on the family's large farm property, which lay at the top of a high, beautiful hill in the district of St. Andres. All the children of Gopinath and Lakshmi Samnaddan-Pillai were there with their offspring. Dozens of small children ran around, enjoying the freedom of the open spaces, where no cars or bicycles threatened to knock them over. They did, however, face the danger of tumbling down the steep hillside and into a ravine, so the adults carefully watched over them.

The dinner had been cooked outside, on large pots over open fires. Tents had been set up with tables and chairs, but, because it was such a large gathering, the guests had to eat in shifts. This was a common practice in Trinidadian East Indian weddings at that time, since so many relatives had to be invited, as well as neighbours and co-workers. It was a remnant of their Indian cultural past, where it was the custom to invite the whole village as well as distant relatives in far-off villages to any family wedding.

The meal was rice and *roti*, curried goat, *dahl*, curried vegetables, and a chickpea dish called *channa*. There were the East Indian relishes of *kuchela* and *anchar* made from green mangoes or the local *pommecythere* fruit, mango chutney, and hot pepper sauce. After the meal, the guests sat in the great room of the large farmhouse while the young people danced to the music of the latest tunes on a gramophone.

Uncle Lou's son, Thomas, had secured the loan of a generator from his workplace to supply light for the reception, for as yet there was no electricity in St. Andres. The light acquired for this occasion was made possible through the generosity of Thomas's boss, Louis de Laurier, a descendant of one of the oldest and most prosperous French Creole families in the island. Out of courtesy, the De Laurier family had been issued an invitation as well. They sent their son Sam—a handsome, young, blond man of twenty—to represent them. Almost immediately, Sam picked out Camille from the bevy of beautiful young girls present. He spent the whole evening sitting next to her and dancing exclusively with her, to the horror of the older ladies. Camille laughed a lot all evening and was openly enjoying the attention of this stranger, so polished and courteous, so different from the young East Indian boys she usually met at family weddings. Camille had never met a young man with such fine manners. Because he was a guest and the son of the man who had supplied them with electricity for the celebration, she felt an obligation to be nice to him.

Tessa was eavesdropping and heard Sam say to Camille, "What beautiful eyes you have. So dark and deep. And your hair, it's so thick and black and shiny." And he was trying to hold her hand, but Camille, keenly aware of the sharp eyes of the older ladies, especially her mother, soon pulled it away. Later Tessa heard Sam say to Camille, "I have to see you again. I want to know your phone number, so I can take you out somewhere."

But Camille only laughed coquettishly and said, "I'm not giving it to you. You better find it out from Thomas."

Tessa thought that Camille was making sure that Sam did not see her as "easy." By not "encouraging" Sam, Camille was behaving the way nice girls were supposed to.

After the wedding celebrations had come and gone, Camille, Tessa, and Sylvia held a post-mortem, as young girls usually did. "Do you think I dared to give him our phone number?" Camille said. "You know how strict my mother is. She doesn't let me go anywhere unless it's to relatives or with my brothers and cousins. And whenever I go to a dance with them they watch me like a hawk and discourage any boy who comes near me. My mother would just go crazy if he came to visit. And I wouldn't be allowed to go out with him anyway," she added with a shrug of her shoulders.

"My mother always says," Camille continued, "that white men with East Indian women are only after one thing. And they would leave you spoiled or pregnant, and go their way."

"What is spoiled?" asked Tessa. She had only heard the word used to refer to children whose parents did not discipline them and who ran wild. Or to food that had gone bad.

"It means when a boy touches you up all over and then boasts to his friends that you are a loose girl," answered Camille. "And then you have a bad reputation, or no reputation at all. Then nice boys will never come around you."

Tessa and Sylvia had never been told about the behaviour that was expected of a "good" girl when she was with boys. Lucille never talked of such things, and, since the girls were never allowed out alone with boys, there was no need to. The nun who was their biology teacher had given them a sketchy and brief description of the male and female sexual organs, but had made no mention of the sexual act and its possible consequences.

After the wedding, Clyde complained to his mother and sisters and to anyone who would listen that because the extended family was so large, family weddings were no place to meet girls. "Every time I dance with a pretty girl, I find out she's a cousin. Sometimes only a second cousin, but Catholics and Hindus forbid marriages between cousins, even second cousins. And though we are Catholic, you and your sisters still act like Hindus. You refuse to eat beef although you don't stop us from eating it; and you cook it for us, but you say you can't swallow it."

The Joseph children thought their mother and aunts old-fashioned because of their refusal to eat beef. They had no idea that the revulsion the older people felt towards eating beef was physical, not merely ethical. Even their conversion to Christianity could not change their physical revulsion to the flesh of the cow.

"Anyway," Sylvia chimed in, after Clyde's diatribe. "I heard that the cousin you fell so hard for is soon going away to Dublin to study so it's just as well, otherwise you'd be making a nuisance of yourself chasing her and getting everybody in the family annoyed at you. And we know her father does a lot of hunting. For they not living too far from the bush, and he have a shotgun, so you better watch out."

"And you know what I hear the other day?" Tessa added. "People say we already have too many second cousins in this family who have got married. The neighbours call us the 'royal family.'"

"What?" Lucille, who had not been paying much attention, suddenly got very interested and indignant. "Which people saying that? Why people always so *farse* in this place? They should mind their own business. At least the girls in our family get married and don't go around having children for different men." But, in the past, her children had heard her pronounce severe judgement on cousins falling in love and marrying.

Clyde replied, "That is because you people so strict about us going out and dating. And you disapprove of girls and boys coming from a lower class than ours, if they living in a slum area and what kind of house they live in and all that. What you expect?"

"Yes, that's true," said Sylvia. "And your best friend, Mrs. Ali, didn't like Henry going out with that half-Portuguese, half-Indian girl. She wasn't pretty, Mrs. Ali said. So then he went to the States and marry a Black girl. I wonder how she liked that. She always controlled her children's lives. Now they have all gone away and can do what they please."

One day, Tessa and Sylvia, intending to make fun of their mother, whom they regarded as belonging to an outdated past, enquired mischievously, "Mom, we want to know how you and your sisters ever got married if your parents didn't let you go to fetes and dances, and they didn't arrange marriages for you either."

Whenever her children tried to denigrate her youthful years, spent in the little village at the edge of the city of Port of Spain, Lucille would say that it was a happy peaceful time, safe and comfortable, not like the world they lived in now. The children never valued Lucille's stories about her childhood and youth. When she talked about the South Indian firepass ceremony that had been held in the village, they looked down on it as part of their family's old pagan religion, before they were converted to Christianity. They were appalled when they imagined this strange ceremony—people walking over hot coals. They didn't know that the participants had not only fasted and prayed before attempting the feat, but had also soaked their feet in the river for hours before walking on the hot coals. In later years, when they read that highly reputable corporations in the United States were evaluating the members of their management team on the basis of their ability to walk over a bed of hot coals, Tessa and Sylvia regretted not listening more carefully to their mother's first-hand knowledge of this ancient tradition.

"Who tell you we didn't go out?" she countered defensively. "Our father would take us to the races at the Queen's Park Savannah, and there the young men would see us and find out who we were and would write a letter asking for us."

That brought a hoot from the two girls, secure in their new modernity, the fast world of the 1950s. "You mean that they would write a letter?" they asked incredulously.

Lucille continued, reminiscing, "That day I met your father, it was Aunt Violet, Aunt Clarissa, and myself. We were the closest in age. We saw these three young fellers looking at us. We didn't know them. They were not from de Gannes village, but Peru village, now San Juan de la Pina. Those were the two East Indian villages in the city. I suppose they found out our names from some of the young men in our village. The story went that Joe, Aunt Clarissa's husband knew she was the one he wanted, and made sure to get her name right." The girls were amused at this recollection. Seeing a girl and deciding she was the one? This was slightly better than how marriages were arranged in the country villages on the island. In the country, the boys and girls would choose partners by merely looking at photographs and never actually meeting each other before the wedding.

Lucille became pensive, remembering the carefree years of her youth. Before marriage, children, responsibilities, death, and widowhood had changed everything. But she launched into the story of how she, Aunt Violet, and Aunt Clarissa had met their husbands.

"I was sixteen, and your aunts, Violet and Clarissa, were seventeen and eighteen. Our father had taken us on Boxing Day, in his horse and cart to the Queen's Park Savannah, to the races. The Savannah was exciting with colour, noise and activity. There were some East Indian women dressed in beautiful *saris* of bright colours, while the poorer ones wore only *orhinis* over their heads and long skirts down to their ankles. All the women, though, wore gold and silver necklaces, and jangling bracelets on their arms, and their ankles were adorned with gold and silver anklets.

"There were penny games set up near the tracks for those who could not afford to bet on the horses, so that they could still have a chance to come away with a prize or two. A man who was nicknamed 'Penny a Mile' walked around the grounds of the savannah, selling freshly roasted peanuts.

"I remember that day as if it were yesterday. It was 1921. The white women, who were coming out of these low, brightly-coloured sporty cars headed for the stands where they would be seated in comfort to watch the races. I saw how they sailed past the common people on the grounds—who were all Blacks and East Indians—not even giving us a second glance. I remember how we marvelled at the dresses those women were wearing; they were made from the finest of materials, and they draped softly and hung close over their bodies, falling just below the knee. All their dresses were sleeveless. Long strings of beads hung around their necks, and on their wrists were matching bracelets. Some of them wore cloche hats—of course we didn't know that's what the hats were called. We only wondered if these women had come from England or America. They could not be from Trinidad, we said to each other. And the shoes. We looked in amazement at them tottering around in those brightly-coloured high-heeled shoes. We had never seen anyone wearing shoes like that.

"And I remember, too, just as we were still talking about the wonderful clothes we had seen, a Black family— a woman and two children—walked past us. The woman, the boy, and the girl were very well-dressed. They looked like Black copies of the white people. The mother was wearing a dress which, though not as fine as any white woman wore, was in the latest style, narrow and fitting, and of course, short. The woman's hair was straightened and combed in a crisp page-boy style. The boy was in short pants, new you could tell; the little girl was in a frilly blue dress and her shoes were black and shiny Mary Janes with straps buttoned across the instep.

"The Black woman glanced at us, and I saw a scornful look on her face. We were wearing short-sleeved dresses of cheap, flowered cotton and though they were not quite ankle length, they were certainly not as short as those the white women and this Black woman wore, and our shoes were plain brown canvas shoes. Our hair, which had never been cut since childhood, was worn in two coils around our ears. At the woman's disdainful look, I came to realize that not only white people could afford to dress in the latest style, but some Black people could too. At that moment, I promised myself that I, too, would some day get fashionable clothes. Since our sister Violet had recently started sewing classes, I vowed that somehow or other I would inveigle Violet to sew some dresses like these for me. Violet had been enrolled at the Canadian Mission School for young East Indian women and was learning all the fine domestic arts that the East Indian girls were being taught in order to become suitable wives for the Christianized and westernized East Indian boys.

"Violet was the only one of our eleven sisters who had been lucky enough to go to that Archibald Institute, as it was called. And she was starting to pass along to us the arts of cake and pastry making, stews and roasts and other western foods, as well as the fine art of sewing. Violet explained to us the different materials to be bought for fashionable clothes. We learned the names of all the fabrics, the difference between cotton, linen, and silk, and voile, chiffon, and georgette. Violet had learned the art of cutting and basting, how to turn a collar, make seams and darts, and how to make hems and cuffs.

"The white women all had bobbed hair, styled in the latest fashion. I wondered if only East Indians kept their hair long. I vowed to cut mine as soon as I could. I knew I would run into trouble with my parents, and perhaps I might never be able to cut it until I got married. But my greatest resolve was that one day I, too, would dress fashionably and find myself coming out of a bright red or yellow car, like these women.

"But my dream ended suddenly. Just as your father's business had begun to prosper, and we had moved into the large house in Meadowbrook, a sudden heart attack ended his life. When he was at his place of business in town, I had become used to dressing up and going to lunch with the wives of his business partners. We would eat at the China Clipper restaurant, which was in the same building as his store. Now all that was gone. I had lost all my money, and fashionable clothes were out of the question, and cars as well. Even though his business had been in the sale of motorcar parts, the first in the city, I had no car. Even if I had, I wouldn't have known how to drive it. But with enough money, a chauffeur could always be hired." Lucille sighed.

Tessa's voice brought her back to continuing the story of meeting their husbands.

"So these boys saw you, Aunt Violet, and Aunt Clarissa, and wrote letters for each of you, and you agreed to marry them?"

"Well, it wasn't just the young people deciding," their mother continued. "Our parents checked out the boys, to see if they came from families that were decent and respectable and hard-working, and if the boys had good jobs or training. The Hindus always have to match the horoscopes of the two young people before they let them get married, and they had to be of the same caste. But we didn't have anything to do with horoscopes and castes since we had become Catholic. If the boys came from good families, then they would be allowed to come courting, and if the girls didn't like them, they didn't have to marry them. And of course, there was nothing about dowries like the Hindus have. But at least we didn't have any of this 'having to get married' business like is all over the place these days."

Tessa knew that "having to get married" brought interminable shame to everyone, parents, sisters and brothers, and the girl herself. It was a situation in which the boys always came out the winners. One day, in talking about one of his friends who "had to get married," Clyde told his sisters,

"She trap him."

"How you mean, she trap him?" asked sixteen-year-old Tessa.

"Well, she get herself pregnant," answered Clyde.

It was not until years later, when women's liberation movement came along, that Tessa saw the unfairness of this commonly used remark. She was filled with indignation for all those girls who had supposedly "trapped" all those boys into marriage, as if the whole thing were a one-way street. Yet the parents of such "respectable" boys saw the other side of the coin. They knew the girls were often those who understood the benefits of marrying a boy from a higher class, a boy who was attending one of the prestigious high school colleges. The girl herself was generally enrolled in a commercial school to learn typing and shorthand, learning to become a dressmaker, or merely a clerk in a downtown store. Marrying a boy who was highly educated would ensure a higher place in the social hierarchy, and this was a way of "hooking" him. But most of all, the boys' parents considered such girls "loose" and not respectable. There was never any mention of their sons' role in the affair; it was all the fault of the girls.

But sometimes the boys' parents would not allow him to be trapped, and the coward would find a way to escape the noose. There was the case of Diego. He had been a frequent visitor to the houses of respectable girls. He was well thought of because he was a civil servant and wore a shirt and tie to work every day, unlike his brother who looked after and killed the chickens in his parents' back yard, where everyone went to get a chicken for their Sunday pot.

"How is it Diego hasn't come to see us for so long?" Lucille Joseph asked Clyde one day. Clyde, looking somewhat guilty, said he didn't know what had happened to Diego. But in San Juan de la Pina, secrets couldn't be kept for long. Soon, the truth was revealed when Mrs. Stevens came over to the Josephs' house.

"I don't know what to say," she said to Lucille. "You know Anne Marie gone and get herself in trouble." No one ever said "pregnant"—it was a dirty word. "Lord, I work so hard for that girl, washing clothes to pay the fees for the convent, and now she go and do this. I so shame. I don't know what to do."

"Who is the boy?" Lucille asked, whispering. They didn't know Tessa was listening, and she had to strain to hear the name. When Mrs. Stevens told Lucille who it was, Tessa nearly said, "What?" out loud, almost letting the women know she was eavesdropping.

"Is that half-Spanish boy, that Diego. He used to come to the house so nice and respectable, nobody would ever suspect he would do a thing like that."

"And why you don't get them married?" Lucille asked with her usual optimism.

"You know why? He run away, that's why. He take ship for Venezuela. My sons and husband can't even go after him, now." Tessa saw the wild waters of the Gulf of Anaconda rising up between Diego and a forced marriage.

Just as Austen's heroines would have to reject suitors who were not considered good enough or rich enough for them, like poor Anne Eliot in *Persuasion*, the privileged few receiving a high school education were expected to choose partners who were of a certain caliber. They had to have white collar jobs. Or, they had to go away to university, so they could rise in the world. But, above all, they had to be of suitable race. A girl who was light-coloured or brown-skinned should not marry a boy who was Black. One of Tessa's friends, a girl of mixed white and Black blood, and probably Aboriginal or Chinese, too—so mixed up were many of the islanders—told Tessa about her sister's marriage, adding, "He black like coal." Tessa thought that someone like Margaret should not talk like that, when she had Black blood in her veins.

In Tessa's family, the marriage partners had to be East Indian. When Shirley, one of their cousins, disappeared one day, Tessa and Sylvia heard her mother and Aunt Violet "shoo-shooing" about it. The girls stood around, hoping to hear what was going on. They were both now old enough to be told stories about sex and disgrace. Aunt Clarissa finally told them with great disgust. "Shirley run away with that neighbour man, that's what she do. The one who was their yard boy. You ever hear anything like that? The man so bold, to interfere with a decent girl like that."

"What yard boy?" Tessa asked. Now that Shirley had run off with the yard boy, she was afraid that she and Sylvia would not be allowed to go and visit those cousins any more because looking at Aunt Clarissa's face, anyone would have thought the world was coming to an end.

"That Black man who live in the village and works for them. You know, they call him Boysie. I blame the brothers, for they always let him hang around with them. He was always in the house. And he was a nobody. His family was only living in a shack and Arabella family give him a job, and this is how he repay them. Why, that man so much older than Shirley, and he never even went to high school. It's a disgrace to Arabella and to all of us too." Tessa knew that whenever any of the relatives did anything disgraceful, it reflected on the respectability of everyone in the extended family, or so they all thought.

Tessa and Sylvia were shocked and confused at this news. But as they talked about it, they realized that it was not the race difference, but the unsuitability of the match that was a problem. For their cousin Shirley was a high school student while Boysie was an unskilled labourer. All the boys and girls in the family were attending high schools and some had already won *island scholarships*. Winning an island scholarship, only four of which were awarded every year, enabled its recipient to attend Oxford, London, or Cambridge Universities and train to be doctors engineers or scientists. These careers and professions were held up to them as the ultimate prize. They wondered what kind of life Shirley would lead, married to an unskilled labourer like Boysie. He no longer even had a job as her parents would not have anything more to do with them. Tessa, especially, felt sorry for Shirley and hoped that her parents would forgive her and give Boysie back his job.

18.
La Rosière

A S TESSA AND HER CLASSMATES were nearing their senior year, Sister Genevieve told them that they were welcome to come back and visit their old school and bring their husbands with them. "That is," she added, "if you are not ashamed of him." Tessa wondered what kind of husband would be considered one to be ashamed of. She suspected it might be one who was not white enough, or handsome enough, or educated enough, or one who did not have a white-collar job. It didn't matter if a husband was thin and weak-looking as long as he wore a tie and white shirt every day and went to an office job. And, of course, he must not be too black, but should have a brown or light-skinned complexion. Taxi drivers, truck drivers, farmers, labourers on the wharf, none of these were considered acceptable husbands for the Sacred Heart Convent-educated girls. These rules of class stratification were made and enforced by the girls who were the leaders, those who were white or "high brown." These girls were looked up to by all the rest of the students.

Form Five, their final year, saw a change in this attitude. It was the custom to choose a girl who represented the ideals of the convent and whose behaviour most closely resembled that of the Virgin Mary, the person to whom all the girls were taught to emulate. La Rosière would be a girl who was never loud, one who never talked back or broke rules, and of course, one who had never in her five years been "called out" in front of the whole school, even if it was for punctuality or through no fault of her own—perhaps because her parents dropped her to school late, or their breakfast was always late, or she had to walk many miles from the train station. La Rosière would have to be saint-like in demeanour. She would have to be "quiet"—that is, hardly spoke and never lost marks for chatting in class. She would never be a girl who, while riding her bike to school, could be seen riding alongside a boy going in the same direction to the St. Francis College, which was opposite the convent. When this rule was first introduced, Tessa had to ask her prefect, "What if the boy you ride to school with is your cousin?" She and Reginald would often ride alongside each other if they happened to meet en route to school. She didn't know how the nuns could ever enforce such a rule unless someone were to tattle to them. The prefect had looked confused and had had no solution to offer. La Rosière would most probably be a girl who was driven to school in a car by parents or a chauffeur and who had to leave school promptly at three o'clock. Or she would be a girl who would take a bus or taxi home right after school, never walking downtown with other girls to buy an ice cream at Woolworth's, which had recently opened, or hanging around the makeup and jewellery counters at the department stores on Frederick Street. La Rosière would be voted on by the graduating class.

Some days before the voting was to take place, one of the Black girls hastily called a meeting. No one knew how the word had spread that only the Black and East Indian girls were invited or how Stephanie had been granted permission to use a room for her meeting. What could she have told the nuns was the purpose of her meeting? Whatever it was, there they were, in a meeting that excluded those who were white or who considered themselves white. Stephanie was frantic.

"I have just learned," she began, "that the white girls intend to have their own grad party. They are not going to come to ours."

Stephanie continued to elaborate on the significance of this. "It would mean that if she is picked from one of them, we will not have La Rosière at our grad party. We have to make sure that La Rosière is chosen from one of us and not from them."

Tessa wondered why it was so important for La Rosière to be at the grad party. After all, it was a dance, and there would be liquor, and girls in off-the-shoulder dresses showing off their flesh, so why would the La Rosière winner need to be at the grad dance? And what of the ideals that La Rosière was supposed to represent? But it was 1956. A Black government, the first independent government of the island, had just been elected. Political consciousness on the part of the Black people had entered the school, which had once been the bastion of the white ruling class. Once they knew that the white girls intended to stay away from their grad party, the non-white girls showed a united front, and made sure that La Rosière came from their ranks. Tessa wondered whether the white girls, holding their whites-only grad party in some sprawling estate in a prosperous enclave, cared. They could do what they wanted. Nobody was going to insist they had to show up at the school's grad party; the others could have their La Rosière. Tessa wondered what the Virgin Mary must have thought of all of this. Perhaps she, too, didn't really care.

19.
High School Certificate

FOR MONTHS TESSA had been agonizing about going back to school to take the Higher School Certificate, called H.C. On learning that both Rosanna and Ashley planned to return, she felt torn. She was afraid that if she changed her mind and decided not to come back, she might miss the excitement of the graduation ceremony, a ritual recently introduced into the island's schools.

The thought of studying more poetry, Shakespeare, and Jane Austen filled her with excitement, but was it fair that neither Clyde nor Sylvia had had the opportunity to do H.C.? And except for their cousin Reginald, who was in the scholarship class, and the ones who had already won island scholarships and were now studying at universities abroad, all the boys and girls in the family had immediately gone to work after passing their Senior Cambridge Certificate exams. She felt guilty even thinking about continuing school for two more years. Money was no longer an issue since both Clyde and Sylvia were now working as civil servants. But why should she be the privileged one?

Rosanna and Ashley had no such conflicts. Ashley's father was a highly paid senior civil servant. Even though Mrs. De Aguilar might be planning to return to Venezuela, keeping Rosanna in school for two more years would prove no hardship, for they were not poverty stricken.

The school had left it up to their students to decide whether they would go through the graduation exercises, even if they thought they might return for two years of H.C. The Senior Cambridge School Certificate was the all-important one. H.C. was considered an extra, icing on the cake. Few students could afford the luxury of staying in school for two more years. They knew how hard it had been for their parents just to keep them in school for five years, paying the high fees, and having to buy books and uniforms. It was now time to pay their parents back for all their sacrifices. Very few of the white and "high brown," or the Syrian, Chinese, and Portuguese girls were coming back, for they knew they were assured of jobs in the banks and in the private business firms, all of which were owned by the English and French-Creoles. Or in their parents' businesses. Others had plans to marry soon. Two more years of school would be a penance they could do without. And then there were those girls who couldn't wait to go out to work. To be able to buy the latest fashionable clothes with their own money. To dress in a tight-fitting skirt with a white blouse and a suit jacket and high-heeled shoes and work in some air-conditioned government office, perhaps in one of the Ministries, the Inland Revenue Department or the Red House. This was an elegant historic building that housed the all-important documents of births, deaths, and marriages in its ancient, dusty vaults.

But girls like Tessa knew they would have to get higher qualifications than a mere Senior School Certificate if they wanted to "make something of themselves," and if they wanted to rise from the poverty their parents had known. A Higher School Certificate from Cambridge University would give them a head start.

The afternoon in October when it was announced that those wishing to return for H.C. should meet in the Upper Sixth classroom after school, a bunch of excited chattering girls showed up. The room fell silent as soon as Sister Aloysius swept into the room, carefully holding on to the huge beads of the black rosary that hung from her side, ensuring the beads would not clank noisily against the desks, her long white gown swishing noisily behind her.

Sister Aloysius began, "I just want to warn you girls that H.C. will not be easy. You will have to make up your mind to work very hard if you want to pass. So you should think carefully before you undertake this commitment for the next two years."

No one dared to get up and leave. She would be branding herself as lazy, or admitting to being unequal to the job.

Sister Aloysius began to peruse the list. Everyone, except for the extremely bright girls who knew they were bound to do well, sat in fear and trembling. As each girl's name was called, the nun would let her know whether she was accepted or whether she had to await the results of her Senior Cambridge Certificate exams. The exams would be written in December, but results would not come back from Cambridge University until late March. The rejected girls had to get up from their seats and under the pitying stares of everyone, walk out of the room. What humiliation, Tessa thought.

When she reached Tessa's name, Sister Aloysius said scornfully, "You? No, I don't think so. You should wait for results."

Tessa was flabbergasted. Me? Again? You mean she's after me again? Tessa thought. And to think that she would accept Vanessa Wilkins and Georgina Mason and not me. They never answer any questions in class. They never get five out of five in English composition. What have I done that this woman, nun or not, hates me so? I'll show her. I'll do so well that she will have to eat her words. Tessa was furious.

But her bravado was only inside. And Tessa still had to get up and walk out of the room.

When results came back and Tessa had to be admitted into the H.C. class, Sister Aloysius was one of her teachers. She slowly began to acknowledge Tessa's skill with the material. After a few months Sister Aloysius was transferred, and on saying goodbye to the class, her parting words to Tessa were, "Don't give up the literature, Tessa."

So, she finally had to eat crow, thought Tessa. But it was too little, too late.

20.
Harvest Festival

THE ANNUAL CHURCH HARVEST festival was being held in the San Juan de la Pina School. The Irish priests had brought the northern custom of harvest festivals to these tropical islands, where crops and fruits of different varieties could be harvested at any time of the year, and where there was no autumn harvest time. Some of the sugar estates held dances for the white residents. These dances were called Crop Over dances And the workers, too, got bonuses and held their own celebrations. But the Church Harvest Festival customs that the islanders had adopted did not celebrate the harvesting of the sugarcane or cocoa or rice, or any local crops. They were merely following the customs of the Irish and English priests.

Some of Clyde's friends from school who also attended the parish church had booked a table and had invited Tessa, Rosanna, and Ashley to join them for the meal. It was a really grown-up thing to do, and, since it was a church function, none of the parents had any objections. Dating was an American custom, and it was not part of the island's culture. Boys and girls going out in groups was all right—there was safety in numbers. Being seen anywhere around town or at the cinema alone with a boy was frowned upon. Especially "around the Savannah," where it was reputed that men and women would go to "the hollow" to "do it." Being seen "around the Savannah" blackened a girl's character, and she would immediately be branded as "loose."

On the day of the festival, the school had been transformed. Desks had been cleared out, and tables had been brought in and laid with white tablecloths. There were stalls offering various kinds of sweets and food for sale. Tessa, Ashley, and Rosanna walked together to the school where the boys were already seated at a table. Most of the regular parishioners were there. There was Miss O'Grady, a tall, ancient, Black woman with an erect back who attended Mass faithfully every morning and who looked after the flowers, the priest's vestments, and the altar cloths. It was rumoured that because she had no immediate family she would leave her property to the church. Though she lived in an old wooden shack, it sat on a generous piece of land.

There were the Singhs, who had recently converted to Catholicism, because the father had said that becoming Christian was the only way to advance in the world. Mr. Singh had one of the lowliest jobs in the community. He was a road sweeper. The Singhs stood out among the regular parishioners because the mother would not give up her *orhini*, the traditional veil Hindu women wore with their ankle-length western dresses. The six Singh girls had long hair that always seemed overly greased with coconut oil and hung down their backs, and they all smelled of the heavily-scented blue soap that poor people used to wash their clothes. Lucille was appalled at the Singhs' "backwardness" and often said this to her children. She did not seem to remember the Bible's exhortation of "Render your heart and not your garment." She had always ensured that she and her children were dressed in the latest styles that they could afford.

To Tessa's surprise, Anne O'Meara, Darlene O'Meara's younger sister, was their server. Darlene had dropped out in Form Four and had secured a job in one of the banks. Because they lived in San Juan de la Pina and attended the same church, Tessa knew all the O'Meara children, and she also knew Anne from school. Tessa's first thought was, why Anne O'Meara?

She was from the parish all right, but so were Ashley and Tessa. As she looked around the room, Tessa realized that the girls who were serving were all white girls from her school. She didn't know why, but she felt humiliated. Was it some kind of prestige to serve at the church supper? She had never thought it was, but then she had never attended any of these. It was an adult activity and neither her mother nor aunts had ever attended one.

Just then Father O'Shaughnessy came over to their table to chat with them. He was a short, rotund, red-faced Irishman. Tessa could not resist. She found herself asking the priest, "Father, how come you have all these convent girls serving at your harvest supper?" She was wondering why the usual ladies who did chores for the church—securing and arranging the flowers, washing and ironing the priest's vestments, and attending Mass every morning—weren't doing the serving? Are they not qualified to serve just because they are not white? Or don't they understand the fine art of serving at a table? All they had to do was to bring a plate of food already assembled and perhaps some glasses of water. The napkins and cutlery were already on the table. Why did one have to be white to do this?

"Oh," Father O'Shaughnessy replied, "those are Sister Philomena's girls. I always get them for my harvest suppers. She tells them what to do and she trains them properly."

Tessa thought, yes, and she only trains the white girls. In all the years I was taking domestic science classes from her, she never asked who attended what parish, so she could recruit them for their church harvest supper.

After the priest had left, Tessa said to the others, "Don't you find it strange that the girls serving are all from the convent?" She didn't add, "And they're all white." All her friends, except for Rosanna, were of mixed race, having Portuguese, Spanish, English, Chinese, and Black blood in their ancestry. Race or colour never entered into their conversations. It had nothing to do with their main goal at this time in their lives, which was having fun. Tessa continued, "Why didn't they ask any of us? We all go to this church except Rosanna."

"Who wants to serve in this hot room anyway?" said Ashley. "It's hard work, and clearing out dirty plates and washing up and all that. I'd rather sit here and enjoy the food, and let them do all the work."

Tessa could not imagine these spoiled little white girls washing up dishes. That would be left to the church ladies, the local parishioners. Ashley's remark was typical of her attitude, she thought. Tessa asked herself why she couldn't be more like Ashley. Why were she and her relatives always worrying about things that other people did not seem to care about? Was it the East Indian inferiority complex that they had? Because they had come to the island after everyone else, and they had strange food, clothes, and religions? Tessa once more found herself vowing that she would make a success of herself in life so that class and race would be forgotten where she was concerned. She had seen how anyone, no matter what his race, who had become rich through business or had made a name for himself in law, medicine, or politics commanded the respect of others. Her Uncle Solomon was a perfect example. He had broken the codes of morality and respectability—he had three wives, one legal, the other two "outside" women—and still everyone kowtowed to him because he was rich.

21.
Getting Out

TWO YEARS IN THE H.C. class turned out to be "the years of plenty," as Tessa later came to regard them. Since Clyde and Sylvia were now working in civil service jobs, Lucille was no longer strapped for money. But it was the activities of the new group that had formed around her, their close-knit friendship, that mattered more to her than the higher income her family had begun to enjoy.

Tessa, Ashley, Rosanna, and the boys with whom they had gone to the harvest supper now met regularly most weekends. In island lingo, such a group was known as a *lime*. No one knew the origin of the term. One theory was that it originated with the English sailors who were called "limeys," a term that came from the ancient sea custom of serving the sailors a daily dose of lime juice in order to ward off scurvy. The *lime* always found something exciting and different to do. There were car trips to the beach or boat trips to the outlying islands—going "down the islands," as it was called. The *lime* hiked to El Tucuche, the highest peak in the island, and visited each other's' homes at Christmas for *ponche* a crème and *black cake*. They even went to the homes of people whom they knew only slightly, for it was Christmas and open hospitality was generally accepted.

The unelected leader of the group was Derek Anderson. Derek's father owned a gambling club on the Main Road of San Juan de la Pina. Downstairs was a pool hall, and upstairs was a night club. He was one of the wealthiest men in the neighbourhood, and he had worked hard to achieve so much. He had started out working on the naval base with the Americans, where he had learned to operate heavy machinery. With his savings, for the Americans paid well, he acquired the valuable property on the Main Road, a growing residential and business district. Knowing how much the American soldiers patronized such places, Mahadeo Anderson, a half-Indian half-Chinese man with an English surname, hit on the money-making venture of a pool hall and a night club, and continued to acquire properties all over the neighbourhood. It was rumoured that he lent out money to those in need and did not hesitate to take over a house from a widow who found herself unable to pay him. Mahadeo Anderson's son, Derek, had won a College Exhibition to Our Lady of Lourdes College, earned a First Grade certificate in the Senior Cambridge exams, and had been a runner-up in the H.C. Island Scholarship exam. He was now working as a civil servant, since his father had not yet agreed to finance his studies abroad.

Reginald Matthews, Tessa's cousin, was also a scholarship student. He was level-headed with a dry sense of humour, and never rattled like Derek. Whenever they were discussing a movie they had seen, Derek would talk about its cinematography, costumes, and direction—things the others didn't care about. And when he did, Tessa and Ashley would nudge each other and grin quietly, but they were too polite to say anything.

Ashley and Reginald had been paired together, and because Reginald was so quiet, the boys began to give him *fatigue*. The word was a local term for teasing, which was often funny but sometimes brutal. The story went that when they had sat on the steps of Ashley's house, all Reginald could find to talk about was the British Constitution, a book he was currently reading. How the others had come to hear about this was debatable.

The third boy was Andrew Lamont, a painfully shy boy who, it was rumoured, was to become a priest, once he felt he had contributed enough to his widowed mother's finances. Rosanna was hopelessly in love with him, but she was afraid that the others would say that it was a sin, because he was going to be married to the church instead of to a woman (she didn't know what constituted a sin since she was not Catholic). She also knew her mother would never approve, since Andrew was not white or even part white. He was a *dougla* with dark skin. Rosanna told Tessa that his quiet personality and his intelligent eyes, which seemed to understand so much, were all the things she loved about him. She said that when she and Andrew sat quietly on the shore while the others were horsing around in the waves, they talked of poetry and Keats and Shakespeare.

They were all musical, thanks to the Irish nuns and priests. It was one of the things that made *lime* so special, Tessa decided. They knew the words to all the songs of the current movie musicals and sang them lustily. But the wit and humour that animated the conversation was never harsh or hurtful. This was something Tessa was to find hard to replicate among the many social groups she would encounter in later life. And the love of singing. It was always something she looked for in friends, and didn't always find. Or found it and then paid a great price. Great guitarists and singers were often the wrong kinds to hang out with, she found out. They offered glamour and excitement, but no stability.

One afternoon after school, leaning on their bikes outside Miss Millie's sweet shop or parlour—where the convent girls went after school to buy tamarind balls, popsicles, and various local sweets—Ashley and Rosanna began talking about where they were going after they finished school. The boys of the neighbouring St. Francis College also hung out at Miss Millie's sweet shop, and though it was out of bounds for the convent girls, it was tucked away on a side street, away from the censoring and prying eyes of the nuns.

Ashley was sure of her plans. "After I finish H.C., I'll be going to England, to London, where my aunt and uncle are living. My uncle is a doctor, my aunt a nurse. I will stay with them until I get into nursing school. And you? Where will you be going?"

Tessa had no answer. She was embarrassed that Ashley would even ask her, knowing Tessa's family's financial situation. But that was Ashley's nature. Perhaps this was why they had remained friends. Ashley was non-judgmental; she never noticed the things that Tessa was always worrying about, and she laughed a lot when things went wrong, while Tessa would be inclined to cry. The day Sister Aloysius had told Tessa she had to await results before she could be admitted into the H.C. class, Tessa had been mortally humiliated. She later found out that Ashley, who never studied much, had been told the same, but she had shrugged it off, in true Ashley fashion.

Rosanna, too, was sure of her plans. "We're going to live in Caracas. Mama thinks we are sure to get well-paying jobs with one of the American or English oil companies there, since we can speak both English and Spanish. She really wants to be able to speak Spanish again. She feels lonely here."

Listening to them talk, Tessa realized that unlike her friends, her family had no connections to the places where everyone was heading for university education. The few cousins who were abroad were struggling students and they could be of no help. Tessa began to think long and hard about how she, too, could go away. Going away was the prestigious thing to do. It meant that you had ambitions, were going to "make something of yourself," and not stagnate on the island.

But was it an impossible dream? Without any access to funds how could she even think of "going away" like her friends? Feeling like she was going around in circles, and that she was always ended up back where she had started from, she almost gave up the idea of going away to study. When Tessa saw an ad in the paper inviting applications for scholarships to universities in India, however, she began to toy with the idea that this might be the solution to her problem. The wild idea of applying went through her mind. The Indian government offered these scholarships because of the thousands from India who had come to the island as indentured agricultural workers from the mid-nineteenth to the early twentieth centuries. She had heard of these scholarships before. She knew someone in her neighbourhood, the sister of a girl who attended her school, who had received one. But they were Hindu people. Would the screening board be broad-minded enough to give it to someone like herself, a non-Hindu?

Tessa consulted Clyde on the idea of applying for one of the scholarships to India.

"I don't see any harm in trying," he encouraged her. "What you have to lose? You never know, you might succeed."

Tessa was surprised that he had not laughed at the idea. He hadn't said, "India? That dirty place?" Instead, he reminded her, "Remember Tanya Lutchman, our Presbyterian cousin from down south who went there, last year? And she didn't run back home. She's still in India. If she could succeed there, I don't see why you couldn't manage, too."

Tessa hoped desperately that she would be one of the winners. But she worried that her miniscule knowledge of India and her westernized and Christian upbringing might prove a problem. Who knew what she would be getting herself into? On the other hand, she mused, if the country of India were to be judged by some of the Indians who lived in the island, it would be considered a backward place, less advanced than our Caribbean island, as small as it is. City people in Trinidad laughed at the way the Indians in the country spoke English, and the calypsonians made fun of them in their songs, but Tessa was sure that the people she would meet at the university would be different from Trinidadian Indians. After all, she rationalized, they would be more like Dr. and Mrs. Sundarsingh—cultured, educated, and soft-spoken—while the young people would be like her childhood friend Sumeera. She would be in a university environment, not among peasants and uneducated people.

But wouldn't going to India be risking failure? For unlike her friends who were heading to England, Canada, or the United States—countries with a western lifestyle—she would, instead, be plunged into a whole new world. Suppose it was so miserable or so inhospitable that she had to return home? Since the scholarship did not promise travel money to and from India, her mother would have to find the large sum to send her there. Tessa's salary was not very high, and she contributed to the household expenses, which didn't leave very much after buying fashionable clothes and shoes and cosmetics, the things she could never afford to have before. And what if her mother were to put out all this money, and then have to fork out more to bring her back before she completed her four years? Tessa had not even won the scholarship and already she was worrying about the cost of travel as well as the possibility of failure.

Tessa knew that if she stayed on the island, her only options would be teaching in hot, crowded elementary schools, under appalling conditions, or pushing papers in the civil service. Though both careers were poorly paid, they ensured pensions and regular salaries.

Some time after she had applied for the Indian government scholarship, and was still waiting in agony to hear whether she had succeeded, the family was sitting and talking in the drawing room after dinner, as was their custom. Soon Clyde came in with Derek Anderson and Reginald Matthews. The drawing room, as it was called in the English tradition, as small and poky as it was, was often filled with the *lime* as well as with other young people who were allowed to join in their tight group. They played cards on the weekends, joked and "gave *fatigue*." Clyde also began a group he called a "salon," which was made up of boys from church and from his old college. They discussed the writings of the fathers of the church, St. Thomas Aquinas, and St. Augustine, as well as Greek philosophers like Aristotle and Plato.

One of the most heated discussions concerned the great debate between a local Catholic priest, Dom Basil Matthews, and Dr. Eric Williams, who was intending to start a political party with a view to ending British control of the island. The wily and erudite Dr. Williams had demolished the good priest's arguments and had craftily turned a debate on education into admiration for the Athenian system of democracy. The debate, originally on education, had degenerated into a debate on slavery. Eric Williams was beginning his quest for the prime ministerial position on the island.

Sometimes the *lime* would walk down the Main Road to buy roast corn, cooked on the grill of an iron cooker fired with charcoal. But Tessa preferred the boiled corn since it was cooked with salt pork, black pepper, onions, and herbs such as thyme and parsley as well as hot peppers, and it had an aroma that was never found in any other food. Or perhaps they would buy *roti* for which the Main Road had recently become famous

On Friday and Saturday nights, the Main Road would be filled with worshippers listening to the preaching of the Baptist or "Shouter" religion. The ministers and their followers would be dressed in long spotless white gowns and their podiums would be lit with the flames of flambeaux. These were bottles filled with kerosene into which a cloth wick would be inserted and lit.

The San Juan de la Pina Main Road on Fridays and Saturdays exuded an air of festivity from the chanting and preaching, and the crowds surrounding the preachers. The Baptist and Shouter followers were mostly from the lower classes and were looked down upon by the Christians of the mainline churches. There were strains of voodoo and black magic attributed to their religions, and Tessa felt that the shouting—and sometimes rolling on the ground and "catching the spirit"—was not very dignified. She was glad that her own church was more sedate and quiet.

Tonight, however, there was no inclination to walk down the Main Road, and the conversation was less ethereal than those of the salon discussions. The three young men, all civil servants, were letting off steam.

"It's a dog-eat-dog world out there," Derek said. "The people you work with always undermining you so that they could get promotions. I can't wait to get out of there."

Derek was biding his time in the General Post Office, waiting for his wealthy but tight-fisted father to release the funds for him to go abroad to university.

Clyde said, "That is not half of it. You know what worse than that? All the talk these days is that from now on, only Black people could expect to get ahead in the Service. They could stick you in a Senior Clerk position for as long as they want and you couldn't do anything about it."

On listening to these fledgling civil servants, Tessa found herself getting more and more depressed. "Why people like us always have to struggle? To think of how hard we all had to work to get not only our Cambridge Senior Certificates, but also Higher School Certificates, and the sacrifices our parents made so that we would be better educated than they were. And now to endure a new kind of suffering in our working worlds? What was the use of all that we went through? Everyone thought that becoming civil servants or teachers, instead of labourers and farmers, would give us a more comfortable life. It might be easier on the body and the hands, but it takes another kind of toll, one on the soul, Tessa thought, as she listened to all the political and social ramifications of their positions. There was prejudice from some of the white administrators and underhanded politicking from some of their Black colleagues. "We're caught in the middle," Tessa reflected.

Reginald, who always watched his words carefully and never ventured an opinion unless he knew what he was talking about, added, "Everybody knows that the banks and the downtown business firms only give jobs to the whites, high brown mulattoes, and Chinese people. So if the civil service and teaching, too, have no future for Indians, where will people like us find jobs now?"

Tessa was nineteen, had obtained a Cambridge Higher School certificate, and was working as a teacher. Everyone she knew was looking forward to going away to university, and because she was always interested in political and social issues—always hotly debating every idea that others put forward, refusing to accept them without question—many people said that the law was the right career for her. But she knew there was no money to send her to England to study at the Inns of Court, so she thought it was a ridiculous suggestion.

That night, Derek, who was always giving advice to younger people about how they could advance in the world, offered Tessa an unexpected alternative, as though he had read her mind.

"You know what I hear today?" Derek began. "It was in the office I heard this. And the people who told me should know. It's that Canada has a new program out in the Caribbean and is now recruiting female immigrants to work as domestic servants. You should try and apply. It's a great opportunity to get into the country and after your term is over, you could go to university and become whatever you want."

Tessa was excited at this piece of news. Since she had little faith she would win the scholarship to India, she thought, why not? This might be an alternative, something to explore if she didn't get the scholarship. Derek's suggestion provoked a stinging reply from Reginald.

"Do you really expect Tessa to work as a domestic, with all her education?" he asked. Tessa was humiliated. She said nothing. She had a great respect for Reginald's opinion and wondered whether Derek's proposal wasn't outrageous. Derek was from a family that always spoke in a "bombastic" way, another one of Tessa's mother's favourite words. The Anderson family looked down on people who were not successful and made fun of them. Though everyone thought that Derek was in love with Tessa, she did not find him attractive and was influenced by what her mother, Lucille, thought about his family. Lucille said that Derek's mother was so thin and sad looking because her husband was not kind to her. He would bring his business and drinking buddies to their home at eleven o'clock at night, and she would then have to make a meal of curried meat and knead the dough for *rotis*. Lucille was appalled at such behaviour, and she thought that Monica Anderson should stand up for herself more than she did and not let her husband trample on her so much. And Lucille often commented on how poorly dressed Mrs. Anderson was when she went to church. It was as if she had just thrown on what had been picked up from the floor, and she wore, instead of proper shoes, sling-back flip flops—not at all suitable for church. Mahadeo Anderson was the worst kind of man anyone could have for a husband, Lucille said, for money was not everything.

Yet at Derek's suggestion, Tessa was seriously tempted. What did it matter that she hated housework? If she were honest with herself, she would not really think of being a nanny. She had not been around children for ten years when she had helped look after Aunt Josephine's baby. But immigration to Canada! It was not to be sneered at. So what if her education had been an English classical one? So what if she had studied Milton and Shakespeare and the Romantic poets and three foreign languages? She would have to swallow her pride and bear the indignity. But for how long? A year and a half? Or five years? Five years would be a most ironic number since that was the length of time her ancestors had been indentured as "bound *coolies*" when they came from India to Trinidad.

Was it the deep-seated class structure of Trinidad, the "What will people say?" syndrome, that made her reject Derek's suggestion? The inner voice that told her that she, a girl with a convent education and an H.C. from Cambridge University, should not demean herself to become a domestic servant?

Derek pointed out that if Sumintra, the sister of their cousin Doug's wife, had gone to Canada as a domestic, why shouldn't Tessa go too?

"You mean to tell me that Sumintra, Doug's sister-in-law actually went to Canada as a domestic?" Reginald asked in disbelief. "And that just because Sumintra, who come from this important Indian family, didn't see anything wrong in going to Canada as a domestic that it's all right for Tessa to go too? Is that what you saying?"

Reginald knew that he was just as bright as Derek, for he too had been a runner-up in the island scholarship exam. While Derek had been in science, Reginald was an English literature student and a top debater, so he had no qualms about challenging Derek.

Before Derek could think of anything to say, Reginald continued, "I remember how Doug's wife's family, those Brahmin Hindu people objected to their daughter Sushila marrying Doug, because he was a Christian. That their grandfather had been a 'priestly pundit, and so they were from the "priestly caste," while we didn't even know what caste we were from. We don't even have our family's letters of indentureship because one of the sisters-in-law threw them out. On his death bed, our grandfather on our mother's side had asked his children to revert to the family name, which had been changed because it was too long. The immigration officers couldn't manage the strange South Indian names, and so Samnaddan-Pillai became Sammy. We found out later that the name belonged to a higher caste in South India. But what difference did his caste make when our grandfather had to cut grass and sell it to the white people for their horses?" Reginald thought he should save Tessa from the disgusting prospect of going as a domestic to Canada.

"Those Brahmin Hindu people wouldn't even come to the wedding, and they let her sister go as a domestic to Canada? Wouldn't that be against their caste?" asked Tessa.

Reginald found the situation incredibly hypocritical.

Sylvia put in her two cents. "You remember, Tessa, how it was Aunt Amelia who had to do the whole wedding for Sushila? She arranged for the church and the priest, cooked all the food, sewed the wedding dress, and got Aunt Violet to make the cake—all things a bride's mother is supposed to do, not the mother-in-law."

"Oh, yes, I remember," said Tessa. "And you were asked to be a bridesmaid for a girl you didn't know. Anyway, haven't all the Brahmins already lost caste after crossing the Kala Pani from India to Trinidad?" she asked, a touch of disgust in her voice. "I don't understand why they still believe in this outdated idea of caste, in this western country. Some of them were not real Brahmins to begin with, whatever Brahmin means. You know that so many of them who call themselves Maharaj have no right to that name? A lot of them took high caste names if there was nobody else from their village in India in the estate they were going to, so nobody would know their real caste once they got there."

Thinking about Derek's suggestion, and Reginald's objections, Tessa found herself remembering her cousin Dominique. It was Derek who had encouraged Dominique to take a job as a sailor on one of the many ships that called at Port of Spain, a thriving port city. Dominique had failed his Cambridge Senior certificate exams, and there was nowhere for him to go. Derek had advised him that it would be better to become a sailor on a ship and come home with a fortune than remain in Trinidad where he could never acquire a decent job and be part of middle-class white-collar respectability.

After a year at sea, Dominique was killed in an accident. It was Tessa's first experience with death in the family. She came home from school for lunch, and everyone was unusually quiet. They waited till she had finished her lunch before giving her the news. It was then she noticed that her mother was not in her "home clothes" and was not puttering about the kitchen as she usually was at lunch time. Her mother told her that all of them would be going to Uncle Lou and Aunt Millicent's, Dominique's parents, and that she could miss school and come with them.

All she could think of now was how as a small child she had been carried on Dominique's shoulders up and down the hills of St. Andres. Uncle Lou and his wife Aunt Millicent were the only ones in the extended family to still maintain a rural life style. They lived in an acreage atop a beautiful hill in the Northern Range not far from the city, kept cows, and grew various food crops. They had a large rambling country house, and Tessa had spent many happy school vacations there, for besides Dominique there were many adult male cousins who picked mangoes for them and took the girls down to the nearby river to swim, always looking after them with great care and concern.

After Sylvia returned home, Tessa would often stay behind in the country, for she had begun to love being part of such a large family, the petting and spoiling of the older cousins, and above all, the mysteries of the hills. Dominique would often have to bring her home, riding in front of him on the bar of his bicycle, after her mother had decided that she had spent too many weeks running wild in the hills, eating too many mangoes, bathing too much in the river, and being bitten by too many mosquitoes. Dominique always went with them to the river; he helped to look after them, these city children who could not take care of themselves in the rain forest, who had to be taught to watch out for centipedes and scorpions when they put on their shoes in the morning, had to be held by the hand as they made their way down towards the river on the narrow slippery tracks covered in decaying forest undergrowth.

But it was the long, dark nights that Tessa remembered. After the parents had gone to bed, they would leave the youngsters to play games of All Fours—a card game perhaps played by nobody else in the world except the people of Trinidad—in the lovely old farmhouse kitchen, blackened by the smoke from the Indian-style earthenware *chula*. Sitting at the long wooden kitchen table, with only a kerosene lamp for light, she felt the mysterious embrace of the tropical night reaching through the windows, the hills illuminated only by the stars and moon, for electricity had not yet reached the hills of St. Andres. Dominique's going off to sea meant the end of those nights. There were to be no more long nights of All Fours in the hills of St. Andres.

Dominique's death was the end of her childhood. The other boys—the cousins from town, Aunt Violet's sons, who had also spent vacations there—moved on too, one to England, one to Canada, one to the United States. It was the age of migration, time to say goodbye to the cramped backward islands, to embrace opportunity and education and become part of the exciting and progressive world outside Trinidad. What they did not know then was that they would be saying goodbye to the perpetual sun and easy freedom of the tropical climate, to the accessibility of the open air, the blue-green sea and its ever-present symphonies, and the sharp ridges and spurs of the hills of their childhood, becoming inured to the enclosed stale odours of winter hallways, if not to the smells of steak in passageways, of boiled cabbage and French fries, and the long cold nights of winter. Since it was Derek who had encouraged Dominique to sign up as a sailor, was he not indirectly responsible for Dominique's death?

Tessa began to think that she should not even give Derek's suggestion a second thought. She might end up, if not killed like Dominique, maybe raped or abused by the people she worked for. There must be some other way to get a university education. She had heard that foreign students in Canada could work their way through university, doing menial jobs such as waitressing or cleaning. The boys who could sing and play guitar usually formed bands to sing calypsoes. Others worked as porters on the trains. But Tessa was not sure what she could do. She knew herself well enough to realize that she was not practical like Sylvia. For it was Sylvia who did many of the chores around the house while Tessa was out *liming* with her friends or had her nose stuck in a book.

22.
Self-Government

TESSA TRIED HARD not to believe the rumours that were becoming more and more common. That the new government would favour the Black people on the island and would discriminate against the Indians and other races. For she had grown up believing the myth that their polyglot island showed the world how people of many races could live in peaceful co-existence.

But the day that she took her class to the library, her belief in this peaceful co-existence that the tourist brochures boasted about was rudely shattered.

The librarian, Mrs. O'Connor, was a Black woman. She wielded such an iron hand and terrorized the children so much that, although she succeeded in keeping the library in a pristine state, few children made use of it, and teachers were discouraged from sending them there. That day her complaint to Tessa was, "There are too many children in your class who never return their books on time. Or never at all. It is the teacher's responsibility. You have to do something about it." This was said loudly and in front of the children.

Tessa shot back, "You want me to go to their house and find the books?"

And she turned away and went to the shelves. She was angry at having been baited like that. And annoyed with herself that the children had overheard what amounted to a quarrel between two teachers.

But it did not end there. She was reported to the principal, Mr. Griffith, himself a black man. Tessa was given a harsh warning about her "slackness" at not monitoring the children's library habits closely enough.

The vice principal, Mrs. De Lisle, also a Black woman and a jolly, heavy-set, kindly woman was Tessa's confidante. Tessa, between tears and sobs, related her humiliation at the hands of Mr. Griffith. Angry and hurt, she felt the injustice of her reprimand and how impossible it was to enforce the library rules. For the school was in a poor district and the children were the sons and daughters of poor farmers and fishermen. Fining them for late or no returns would be pointless and unproductive.

"Child, that woman is a racist," was Mrs. De Lisle's attempt at consoling Tessa. "Everybody says that. And everyone also know that she only get this job because she is a great party organizer. Even the scholarship she get to train as a librarian in England is because she do so much for the party. I went to school with her. She wasn't bright at all. She got only a Third Grade Cambridge School Certificate. But this is how it is today here, girl. If you in the party, you can get anything. Me so, I don't belong. Otherwise I'd have been the principal, instead of Mr. Griffith. You notice what kind of English he speaks? The other day on the P.A. system he said, 'breakfasts-ess.' Imagine! A principal saying that. But one thing I telling you, chil'. You would do well to get out of this place. It is well known that the party have no use for Indian people like yourself. They say, 'Is our turn now,' meaning Black people. They say that the Indians got five acres of land after indentureship, but Black people didn't get any compensation for slavery. That is why all yuh Indians have so much money and land today, and we don't have anything."

"What rubbish!" Tessa said indignantly. "All Indians don't have money or land, especially people like us in the city. And many Indians didn't get land like the history books claim. The

British government went back on their promise. And most of the Indians in the country still cutting cane for starvation wages for the big English sugar companies or planting and selling vegetables. And they still living in ol' wooden shacks or mud huts. Without running water or indoor toilets. Or electricity."

But after her conversation with Mrs. De Lisle she realized that there was no point in trying to carve out a career for herself on the island. That if she wanted a better life, she had to leave. She was convinced that there was somewhere in the world where there would be no discrimination on the basis of race. And no bullying. She was sick of being bullied by every other race: whites, high browns, Chinese, and Portuguese. And now the Blacks were beginning to do the same thing to East Indians. But above all, she hated being looked at by non-East Indians as if they were thinking, "What you doing here, *coolie* gal?"

Tessa, with that familiar sick feeling in her stomach, that feeling that came upon her whenever she encountered anything challenging or difficult, decided that no matter what it would be like, she would go to India if she got the scholarship. Though she hardly dared to hope she would win it, she knew it was the only chance she had of getting out. She rationalized, "If I win the scholarship at least I would get to visit a far-off land, the land of my ancestors, and see the Taj Mahal." There had always been a huge, beautiful picture of the Taj in their drawing room, and its magnificence had never ceased to impress everyone, the children who grew up with it and visitors who never failed to comment on it. It had been one of the few things in their house reminding them of their ancestral homeland. One was a small table-sized statue of the Buddha in a cross-legged pose. Another was a small statue of Gandhi. These were the only mementoes of her father that were left. Tessa wondered how many more Indian artifacts he might have purchased if he had lived longer. She knew only one person who had ventured to India, a neighbour's son who had given up a prestigious post at the University of Southern California to become a farmer in India. It must not have worked out, for he had returned to California, and no more news of him had been relayed to the island. Going to India. That alone must be worth something, she thought to herself.

To everyone's surprise, especially her own, she won the scholarship. She was to go to Delhi. The day her picture appeared in the paper with the announcement of the winners, Derek was the first to come over to their house.

They sat in the drawing room with her mother, Clyde, and Sylvia. Immediately, without one word of congratulations, Derek began to question Tessa's decision to accept the scholarship.

"Why you want to go there? To India? To that land of 'the naked fakir' as Churchill called Gandhi? Where people are poorer than here? With noseless and eyeless lepers lining the streets? We have no more lepers in Trinidad. We cured them a long time ago. They closed the leprosarium in Cocorico."

Though her mother would often lambaste Derek and his family to her children in private, she would never let on to the Andersons how she felt about the things they said and did. She remained quiet. For she disliked open disagreements, though privately she would instill in her own children the virtues she thought the Anderson family lacked.

Clyde said, "I think that Tessa is being very brave to go there. And that it's an opportunity she shouldn't turn down. And we have a cousin there. Also in Delhi. In the same women's college that Tessa will be going to. She'll have someone to help her out at first."

"But I hear it's a dirty place," Derek continued. "That the people spit *betel* juice on the streets, wherever they are. And they go to the bathroom wherever they can, for they have no indoor toilets, or toilets of any kind, not even cess pits, and of course no public ones. And you bound to get sick, with all the unsanitary conditions over there. And what about those parents breaking the legs and arms of their children to make them beggars so that the rest of the family can eat?"

This time, Lucille lost her temper. "I don't see why you should be discouraging the chil' so, Derek. Where else she could go? It's the only chance she have. I think she did well to get the scholarship. You should be congratulating her."

But Derek would not stop. He did not sense the hostility they were all feeling towards him. He continued, "In India squatters live in hovels made of scraps of wood and cardboard in the big cities of Delhi, Calcutta, and Bombay, and some of them don't even have that, but sleep on the pavement on bags, if they have any. In Trinidad we only have a few like that downtown, or in the east end of the city, behind the bridge as they call it, in Lancaster Hill," he ranted. "I don't know why you all allowing her to go to a place like that. As the mother and the brother, you should put a stop to it. It's a crazy idea, if you ask me."

It didn't matter to Derek that he himself was not going anywhere. He was still waiting for his father to loosen his purse strings and send him away. After Derek's visit, Tessa began to grow a hard shell and ignore all the negatives about India that everyone began to point out to her. They told her the food was inedible. That they knew boys who had gone mad while there. But the greatest discouragement was that her Indian university degree would not be accepted when she returned. That in the teaching service she would be placed in a lower pay scale than those with degrees from Britain or Canada or the United States. Only degrees from the top universities in Canada and the United States were recognized by the Trinidadian Ministry of Education. The new government wanted everyone to be graduates of English Universities or Ivy League American universities like Princeton, Harvard, or Yale; though an exception was made for Howard, for it was a university for Black Americans. Only top Canadian Universities such as McGill, Toronto, Queen's, or the University of British Columbia were recognized. Degrees from Manitoba, Saskatchewan, Alberta, and smaller provinces were considered inferior.

Realizing that her degree would not be recognized when she

got back, Tessa decided that she would cross that bridge when she got to it. Four years was a long time. By then, hopefully, Indian university degrees would no longer be discriminated against. Or she could return to the island and work and save enough money to go to Canada, Britain, or the United States and get another degree.

"Don't worry," one of the neighbour ladies told her encouragingly. "Perhaps you will marry an Indian prince over there." Tessa laughed, thinking that Indian princes would not be walking on the university campus or along the streets of Delhi where she would be, that they would be more likely to be riding elephants in the forest and shooting tigers. For she had read that after independence, though their states had been taken over by the Indian government, the Maharajahs had been given princely purses, and were still not like ordinary Indians. And that many of them had run for public office and were now in government.

All the negatives began to frighten her. But she decided that others could never understand why she wanted to leave the island, to go away, anywhere, at any cost. They were not as desperate to succeed in life as she was. They had never aspired to know about the art and culture of the wider world outside the island, as she had.

But Tessa was determined to go. There was no way she could turn down the opportunity. Clyde helped her get all the necessary papers together. Before Tessa could apply for a passport, they had to visit a commissioner of oaths and Clyde had to swear an affidavit. It stated that the name Stephanie, which appeared on the certificate, was only a middle name and that the name by which she had been known from birth and which appeared on all her school documents, was really Theresa and not Stephanie. It said that Stephanie and Theresa were one and the same, and that her first name, the name by which she had always been known, was Theresa. And lastly, Clyde had to swear that he made the declaration in good faith.

On noticing on her birth certificate that her date of birth was the twenty-fourth of April and not the fifteenth, the date on which her birthday had always been celebrated, Tessa asked her mother about the discrepancy.

"Well, it was because of how things were in the old days. The old French lady who did the birth and death certificates for the de Gannes village area was a real hog," Lucille Joseph explained. "If we did not report the birth within a day or two, she yelled and screamed and carried on, so your Uncle Cliff, who was sent to register your birth, decided to give her the twenty-fourth as the date of birth so she wouldn't scold him as an ignorant *coolie* for not coming a day or so after the fifteenth. But everybody was always busy and it was sometimes difficult to get to the office right away. Don't forget they had to walk or ride their bikes everywhere. But we always celebrated your birthday on the right day, the fifteenth."

Tessa realized that her parents and relatives must have gone through a lot of misery, being bullied by the old colonial powers for such simple things. The French woman's name was Anne De Villiers. But her handwriting was appalling, a childish scrawl, a third grader would be ashamed of. Tessa thought that this Anne de Villiers must have been a descendant of the woman in *A Tale of Two Cities* who was always knitting names. When the people were guillotined, she would unravel the names. She must not have been from the old aristocratic French families, to have such an illegible scrawl.

Once the passport had been applied for, they had to make the travel arrangements. Clyde and Tessa laughed at the prospect of booking "A Passage to India, for they knew of the illustrious book, and just the thought itself was an awesome one.

23.
Departure

I T WAS THE ORIENTATION session at the office of the High Commissioner for India. The two scholarship students, Tessa and a young man called Anil Sharma, saw a film about the country to which they would be going. Tessa was so overwhelmed at the breathtaking views of the Himalayas, the houseboats on the Dal Lake, the towering pine-clad mountains, the majestic rivers, that she couldn't wait to get there, to experience first-hand all this beauty. When she learned that in the summer holidays, all the scholarship students who would be coming from Southeast Asia, Africa, and the Caribbean to study at universities all over India would be attending camps in resort areas like Kashmir, Darjeeling, and Ootacamund, some of Tessa's fears and tensions quickly evaporated and were replaced by excitement.

Kind relatives began to introduce Tessa to various people from India who were living on the island. One was a woman doctor married to a Trinidadian businessman. On meeting Dr. Mohammed, Tessa was reminded of Mrs. Sundarsigh, the mother of her childhood classmate, Sumeera. Dr. Mohammed spoke with the same refined accented English as Mrs. Sundarsingh, and, best of all, she was from Delhi and could tell Tessa about the university, which she, too, had attended. Tessa went to visit Nina, the sister of a girl she knew at school, who was now back from India. Nina, however, had been in Benares, and Tessa was secretly glad that she would be going to a much bigger centre and wondered how Nina had been able to survive in Benares.

Her cousin Camille took her shopping for clothes, and she bought some fine wool fabric from one of the downtown department stores. Their dressmaker, Sheila, was to make two suits for the Delhi winters. The idea of a suit was new to Tessa. Only the women who worked in the downtown air-conditioned offices wore suits; everyone else wore cool cotton dresses more suited to the hot humid climate. The rest of Tessa's clothes would be cotton dresses, and she would buy some sweaters in England when she stopped off there, to survive the cold but snowless winters she would encounter in Delhi. She wondered how she would feel among all those girls at her college wearing *sarees* and *shalwar-kameezes* where, except for other foreign students, she would be the only one in western clothes. She quickly decided she didn't know how to tie a *saree* anyway, even if she had one, so why was she even worrying about that?

A slate of parties were held for her. One was at their tiny house, where the furniture was pushed back to allow for danc-ing. But the barbeque party given by Aunt Beatrice, who had begun to prosper once she had moved to St. Andres, remained one of the most memorable events in Tessa's life. The house was on top of the same hill as her Aunt Millicent's. The night of the party saw a full smiling moon illuminating the valley. The older people pronounced prophetically that its beams were shedding good luck on Tessa's future. Throughout the evening Tessa found herself wondering whether she would ever find such friends at university. She thought about how, without the support of her cousins and her aunts and uncles, she would be alone. Thoughts like these began to dog her joy at these festivities. Perhaps, she thought, she should just have been allowed to slink away quietly, without all this fuss, in case she had made a dreadful choice. Too late now, common sense intervened. Just enjoy it all, she told herself. You are so lucky to have such good friends and family. They don't have to do this. But partying and socializing was part of the island's culture—why was she choosing to leave all of this behind? The thought nagged at her.

Aunt Violet and Aunt Clarissa invited her for lunch and dinner, and when she had no free time left, Aunt Louisa insisted on breakfast. Her Uncle Solomon, on coming to say goodbye, gave her a lecture, reminding her that she was going there for one reason, and one reason only, and she must never forget it. Tessa and Sylvia later laughed heartily at what they thought was corny and unnecessary advice. After all, wasn't she travelling thousands of miles away? Why would she not remember why she had gone there? Yet Tessa was to find that the words would haunt her throughout her university years when she was in the depths of despair, and when she felt her world was collapsing around her.

On her visit to the convent to say goodbye to her favourite nun, Sister Bernard, her words, too, remained indelibly etched on Tessa's mind for the next four years. As Tessa unburdened herself of the fears of what might lie ahead for her in this distant eastern land, the warnings she had been given about the conditions she would probably meet, and whether her upbringing had prepared her for them, Sister Bernard said, "Oh, when I was teaching in the convent in the south, one of my students, a Presbyterian girl, also won a scholarship to India. She had been brought up like you, in a western environment, and if she was able to survive, surely you will too. She is now teaching at the Mon Repos Girls College run by the Presbyterians."

But it was Sister Bernard's stern warning to Tessa, as well as her Uncle Solomon's words, that never left her during her four years in India. Sister Bernard had said, "You had better stay the course. If you don't, you will be no good for yourself the rest of your life. You are a perfectionist, and always expect the world to be perfect. It is a world in which you will encounter disappointments, betrayals, and heartaches, but you will have to learn to cope with them."

Tessa was flabbergasted at Sister Bernard's words. She never dreamed that Sister Bernard knew so much about her. No one had ever told her that she was a perfectionist, in all the criticisms and moral and ethical guidelines that had been instilled in her. She pondered its significance. Sister Bernard's admonition to "stay the course" echoed through Tessa's mind like a mantra throughout the whole time she was studying in India.

As the S.S. Colombie, on which Tessa was to travel to England to take her plane to India, left the harbour of Port of Spain, she wondered whether she would ever see the island again. Many people did not return after they went away to study. Too often they could not afford to, especially if they married abroad.

But Tessa could not imagine never returning. Never to relax again on the beaches of the North Coast, or to hear the roar of the open Atlantic on the east coast, or to drive through the rain-forested hills when the pink and yellow *poui* trees were in bloom would be a travesty. Never again to feel the throb of the steel drums, to laugh at the raucous wit of the calypsoes, to experience the colour and abandon of Carnival was unthinkable. Never to see again the faces of her friends and relatives and especially her mother, sister, and brother, who loved her and had taught her to be brave and follow her impossible dreams, was not to be imagined.

At the same time, there was excitement at the thought of what lay ahead. The whole world was now open to her. She would be able, once her studies were over, to visit all the countries of the world that she had only studied in her geography texts. She could go to Europe and see the art she had only seen pictures of in books. Who knew where she would find herself in the future? And with luck she could return to her beloved island a success, with qualifications enabling her to embrace newer and greater opportunities either on the island or elsewhere. And with her success, she would have a new confidence that would enable her to feel equal to anyone she would encounter.

Acknowledgements

Many people have guided, encouraged, assisted and influenced the writing of this book. My first tentative draft, was, with great trepidation, shown to renowned Caribbean writer, Lawrence Scott, while he was writer in residence at the St. Augustine campus of the University of the West Indies. Kathy Page, at the Banff School of Fine Arts and Olive Senior at the Humber College Creative Writing program guided me through the chapters as they came to life. I also owe a debt to H. Nigel Thomas for reading and suggesting changes to my first perfunctory chapters. Margaret Hart of Humber College made very valuable suggestions. The late Dr. Stephen Bennett of horse racing fame was kind enough to describe from first hand knowledge, the racing venue of the Queen's Park Savannah. The late Ben Elliot was invaluable in describing the old days of horse racing as well as supplying details of life in earlier times in the island. Lionel Dwarika recalled important details of the clothing and hairstyles of the older generation of East Indian women. The late Judith Pillai-Procope's thesis on the ancestral village was of great help. Lionel Dwarika and Winston Madray had intimate knowledge of the old-fashioned grocery stores. Farida Lalbiharrie and Ed Deen filled in gaps in my knowledge of the *Hosein* festival and the construction of the *tadjahs*. And thanks to friends such as Noble Lalbiharrie and my book club buddies who read the manuscript and supplied feedback. Cecil Aqui, researcher extraordinaire, never failed to assist me with his extensive computer skills. To all these people I extend grateful thanks.

I also acknowledge the excerpt from "Parades, Parades" from *Selected Poems* by Derek Walcott. Copyright © 2007 by Derek Walcott. Reprinted by permission of Farrar, Straus and Giroux.